PIPPA'S
iSLAND

BOOKS BY BELINDA MURRELL

Pippa's Island

Book 1: The Beach Shack Cafe
Book 2: Cub Reporters
Book 3: Kira Dreaming
Book 4: Camp Castaway
Book 5: Puppy Pandemonium

The Locket of Dreams
The Ruby Talisman
The Ivory Rose
The Forgotten Pearl
The River Charm
The Sequin Star
The Lost Sapphire

The Sun Sword Trilogy

Book 1: The Quest for the Sun Gem
Book 2: The Voyage of the Owl
Book 3: The Snowy Tower

Lulu Bell

Lulu Bell and the Birthday Unicorn
Lulu Bell and the Fairy Penguin
Lulu Bell and the Cubby Fort
Lulu Bell and the Moon Dragon
Lulu Bell and the Circus Pup
Lulu Bell and the Sea Turtle
Lulu Bell and the Tiger Cub
Lulu Bell and the Pyjama Party
Lulu Bell and the Christmas Elf
Lulu Bell and the Koala Joey
Lulu Bell and the Arabian Nights
Lulu Bell and the Magical Garden
Lulu Bell and the Pirate Fun

BOOK 5

PIPPA'S ISLAND

PUPPY PANDEMONIUM

BELINDA MURRELL

RANDOM HOUSE AUSTRALIA

A Random House book
Published by Penguin Random House Australia Pty Ltd
Level 3, 100 Pacific Highway, North Sydney NSW 2060
penguin.com.au

Penguin
Random House
Australia

First published by Random House Australia in 2018

Copyright © Belinda Murrell 2018

Addresses for the Penguin Random House group of companies can be found at
global.penguinrandomhouse.com/offices.

A catalogue record for this
book is available from the
National Library of Australia

ISBN: 978 0 14379 326 7

Cover and internal design by Christabella Designs
Cover and internal images: red vintage bicycle with basket and flowers iofoto/
Shutterstock; young girl in summer park Andrey Arkusha/Shutterstock; happy
children in summer zagorodnaya/Shutterstock; jack russells digging a hole in the
sand at the beach Javier Brosch/Shutterstock; summer icon set vector illustration
Ksenia Lokko/Shutterstock
Typeset by Midland Typesetters, Australia
Printed in Australia by Griffin Press, an accredited ISO AS/NZS 14001:2004
Environmental Management System printer

Penguin Random House Australia uses papers that are natural, renewable
and recyclable products and made from wood grown in sustainable forests.
The logging and manufacturing processes are expected to conform to the
environmental regulations of the country of origin.

For Ava, a sassy girl who is 'strong, smart, brave and . . .' just like Pippa.

Have you ever had that experience when all
your friends have something that you don't?
Something you really, really want? I should
be used to it by now. But try as I might
to ignore it, sometimes it can really bother
me. I guess it's jealousy, and it sneaks in
past my guard like a naughty puppy.

Money has been very tight in our family
for the last few months. Ever since we
moved from London to gorgeous Kira
Island. Well, actually, ever since my dad
left us to go and live in Switzerland. Before
that we lived in a big, rambling terrace
house and we never really noticed money.
When we moved here, Mum spent every
penny we owned on buying and renovating
a dilapidated old boatshed on Kira Cove.

The ground floor has been transformed
into the Beach Shack Cafe, which is now
one of our favourite places to hang out on
the island. The plan was to live upstairs

in an apartment in the attic, but building it has been super-slow. So we are still living, jam-packed, in the old caravan in my grandparents' back garden.

'We' is my family – Mum, my brother Harry, my sister Bella, our golden retriever puppy Summer, and a tiny scrap of a kitten called Smudge. Mimi and Papa have helped us in so many ways – painting the boatshed, looking after us while Mum's at work, puppy-sitting, building furniture, cooking, helping us with our homework and spoiling us to bits. But as much as we love them, none of us can wait for the day when we have our very own home on Kira Island. Most of all, I can't *wait* to have my own bedroom again.

Finally the end is in sight! The builders have been working long days and Mum is totally frazzled working full-time at the cafe and painting at night. Harry, Bella and

I help as much as we can and try not to grumble.

Thank goodness for the Sassy Sisters – my gorgeous group of best friends. I've been thinking a lot about friendship lately, and I think a good friend is someone who cares for you and looks out for you, not just in the fun times, but more importantly when things get tough. That's exactly what we do for each other.

Cici can be prickly, but she's the first to make you smile if you're sad, or whip up a batch of your favourite cupcakes. She says cupcakes can fix any drama! Charlie comes from a big family, so she understands how siblings can sometimes drive you totally crazy. And Meg is the perfect listener – always kind, caring and compassionate. She sees the best in everyone.

The girls remind me to 'Be brave! Be bold! And be full of happy spirit!' It's not always easy but it does help me to celebrate all the great things I have, rather than worrying about the things I don't have.

Pippa

CHAPTER 1

THE GREEN-EYED MONSTER

It was super-early on Sunday morning when I was woken by Mum's alarm. The beeping sound was quickly switched off. I could hear Mum creep out of bed, gather some clothes and head out the caravan door to the bathroom in Mimi and Papa's cottage. I peeked through half-closed eyes. It was barely light outside. I rolled over and snuggled back under my doona.

I was just slipping back into lovely sleep,

when I was woken again. This time it was Summer whining and pawing at the door. I waited for someone to let her out, and then realised that the someone would need to be me. I clambered down from my top bunk and checked the time. It was 5.30 am – way too early to be awake on a Sunday morning.

'Come on, girl,' I whispered to Summer as I opened the door. We slipped out into the dewy garden. The early morning air was cool, with the fresh scent of frangipani flowers and wet grass. Summer sniffed around the lemon tree and did a wee. I watched her, shivering slightly in my cotton PJs and bare feet. I gave Summer a pat, then called her back inside.

I'd only been gone a few minutes, but in my absence it looked like a cyclone had struck. Bella was rummaging through the cupboards looking for something. She'd emptied all her drawers on the floor, then Harry's and mine. We only have two drawers each, but still.

My clothes were all crumpled and jumbled with Harry's. Worst of all, my private notebook was lying open on the floor, tossed to one side. I was furious.

'Bella, look what you've done,' I shouted, snatching up my notebook and snapping it shut. 'You've thrown all my stuff on the floor.'

'Well, I can't find my dinosaur tail *anywhere* and I was *trying* to get dressed,' Bella yelled back at me.

'Why would your *stupid* dinosaur tail be in *my* drawers?' I demanded.

'It's *not* stupid and it wasn't in my drawer or Harry's or the wardrobe, so I thought Mum might have put it away there,' Bella roared, as loudly as a raging *Tyrannosaurus rex*.

Our fighting woke Harry in the bottom bunk, who pulled his pillow over his head and groaned.

'Can you *please* be quiet?' he demanded. 'It's the middle of the night. I'm trying to sleep!'

When Mum came back from the shower, dressed ready for work, Bella and I were still shouting at each other. There was mess everywhere and poor Summer and Smudge were cowering together in Summer's bed under the table.

'Pipkin, what on earth is the matter?' asked Mum, gazing around in despair at Bella's destruction.

'It's *not* fair,' I complained. 'Bella's thrown all my stuff everywhere, and she never respects my space or my privacy or my things . . .'

My throat had a huge lump halfway down and my eyes brimmed with hot tears. It can be very trying living with my sister the dinosaur in such a small space.

Mum sighed and turned to Bella.

'And Bella-boo, why did you throw all of Pippa's clothes on the floor?' asked Mum.

'I can't find my dinosaur *tail*,' shrieked Bella,

her voice wobbling dangerously on the last word. 'And I need it.'

Mum sighed again and wiped her face with her hand. She took a deep breath. I think she was silently counting to five.

'Okay, let's get this mess cleaned up,' suggested Mum in a forced cheery tone. 'And then we'll see if we can solve the mystery of the missing dino tail.'

Mum tried to cajole us out of our cross moods as we picked up all the clothes, books, toys and Harry's magic equipment.

'It won't be long now until the apartment is finished,' Mum assured us. 'Then you'll all have your own rooms again.'

'You've been saying that for ages,' I growled, 'but the builders are *sooo* slow.'

'They do have other jobs to work on as well as ours, Pipkin,' replied Mum.

Actually, the builders had only just started working on our apartment again a week ago after a whole month working on another job. I'd overheard Mum telling Mimi that she'd had to let them have a break until she could afford to pay them.

We sorted the clothes into piles and refolded them, before stacking them neatly in the different drawers. Harry and I made our beds, one above the other. Mum's number one caravan rule was that all bunks must be made neatly every morning. She made up the double bed that she shared with Bella. It was a knotted tangle of sheets, doona and teddy bears.

'And look what I've found, Bella-boo,' said Mum triumphantly, as she extracted a fluffy green appendage from the bottom of the rumpled doona. 'The missing dino tail.'

Bella cuddled the tail and then put it on. I rolled my eyes at Harry. All this fuss for nothing. My sister can be such a drama queen.

At last the caravan was returned to normality and I gave Summer and Smudge a big snuggle.

Puppies and kittens hate shouting. Cuddling them made me feel a little better too.

By this stage, Mum was running very late. The cafe is open seven days a week from 7 am to 5 pm, and Sunday breakfast is one of the busiest times, so she is usually at work by six o'clock to set up. Eventually Mum plans to employ more staff to share the work, but she can't quite afford that yet.

After all the early morning mayhem and tidying up, it was no wonder I was feeling tired and grumpy. The weather today seemed to match my mood perfectly. It was windy, grey and cloudy, and the air smelled of impending rain. So when Cici rang to ask me to come over with the other girls for a lazy afternoon of Sassy Sister bonding and movie watching, I was certain my day was looking up.

Later that afternoon, I walked over to Cici's house to meet the others. Charlie and Meg rode their bikes. I don't have a bike because Mum sold ours back in London. I felt a twinge of envy as Charlie sailed up on her red, vintage-style bicycle. It had a wicker basket on the front which looked perfect for carrying bunches of wildflowers or French baguettes. I wished I had one just like it.

'Hi, Pippa,' called Charlie and Meg together, as they swung off their bikes and parked them out the front.

'Hi, Charlie. Hi, Meg,' I replied.

Cici flung open the door and ushered us inside her mum's studio. Her dog, Muffin, came bounding up to say hello.

'Come in. Come in,' Cici said, beaming in welcome. 'Mum and Dad are in the kitchen.'

I gazed around the design studio with its large antique table, the two headless manne- quins, which were currently wearing silver sequined evening dresses, and the large mood board covered with its ever-changing array of swatches, sketches and photographs.

'When did your mum get home?' asked Charlie.

'She came back yesterday afternoon, *finally*,' said Cici. 'We picked her up from the ferry.' Cici's mum, Nathalie, is a fashion designer who travels a lot for work. This can be hard for Cici and her brother, Will, because they miss her a lot when she's away. This trip had been particularly tough because Nathalie had been away for two whole weeks, visiting boutiques, department stores and suppliers in Melbourne and Sydney.

'Did you do something fun last night?' asked Meg.

'Dad cooked a big welcome-home feast with all Mum's favourites, like duck pancakes, prawn dumplings and ginger-soy barbecued pork. Then we watched a movie and Mum let us stay up late.'

'That sounds delicious,' I said. We all loved Eric's cooking. He was a brilliant chef and could cook anything, but amazing desserts were his specialty.

We all went out the back to say hello to Cici's parents, who were sitting at the kitchen bench doing the word puzzles in the newspaper. The kitchen, as always, smelled warm and welcoming. Today I could smell caramel and exotic spices. Nathalie was so pleased to see us all. She asked endless questions about school and sport and our parents and siblings. Though nothing much had changed while she'd been away.

'And you still haven't moved into your apartment, Pippa?' she asked me.

I shook my head despondently. 'No.'

'I'm sure it won't be long now,' she said warmly. 'Don't forget to give my love to your mum and ask her if there's anything we can do to help.'

We finally escaped into Cici's bedroom, or her 'boudoir' as she likes to call it, all of us talking at once. Cici's room is absolutely gorgeous, decorated in mossy greens and turquoise with pops of hot-pink and orange. It's like a room out of a magazine (I should know – I've been flicking through piles of Mum's interior design magazines looking for ideas for my own dream bedroom). There are quirky decorations such as a fake reindeer head wearing an orange scarf and a heart-shaped mood board crowded with polaroid photos of Muffin and Cici's family and, of course, loads of the four of us together. Picture windows draped with filmy curtains overlook the garden, and in pride of place is the long bank of built-in wardrobes, overflowing with the most adorable clothes, shoes, jewellery and accessories.

The afternoon started well as we lay around listening to music, painting our fingernails and chatting about our week. Normally this is one of my favourite things to do. But today I was feeling cantankerous, and I told the girls all about my early morning wakeup call, describing the mess and the noise.

'And after all that fuss the stupid tail was at the bottom of her bed the whole time,' I exclaimed. 'My sister drives me crazy!'

'Poor Pippa,' said Meg. 'It must be hard living in a tiny caravan.'

Meg lives in a yacht, so she does know what it's like, but everyone in her family is tidy, so it doesn't drive her mad living in such a small space.

'My sister Daisy is always messing up my things too,' said Charlie, fluttering her lavender nails to dry them. 'Sophia thinks we should put tape on the floor to mark off Daisy's third of our bedroom so she's not allowed to cross into our sections. But of course Daisy would *never* take any notice of it.'

Charlie shares a bedroom with her sister, Sophia, and her half-sister, Daisy. She also has two stepbrothers, Seb and Oscar, who can sometimes be noisy and annoying, but fun too. Charlie loves living in such a big, chaotic family.

'I wouldn't have much luck marking a line to show Bella's share of the caravan,' I joked, enjoying the sympathy from my friends. 'She only has half of Mum's bed.'

'Our house is totally quiet compared to you guys,' said Cici. 'Especially this week when Mum was away.'

Cici was sprawled on her bed with Muffin beside her, while Meg and I were sitting on cushions on the floor, rummaging through the box of nail polish.

'Navy or green?' I asked the girls, holding up two shimmering bottles.

'Try green for a change,' said Charlie.

I took her advice and started painting my toenails a glossy mint-green.

'I'm going orange this time,' said Cici, holding up one hand with bright citrus-coloured nails. 'It's my new favourite colour.'

'Did your mum bring you back anything from her trip?' asked Charlie, who was curled up in the armchair in the corner with foam plugs between her toes to stop the nail polish from smudging.

Cici's mum almost always brings back lovely presents for Cici and Will, like the jewelled sandals she bought in Italy a few months ago. Cici managed to enjoy them for just a couple of days before Summer discovered them in my bag and destroyed them. That disaster was definitely one of my worst memories of Kira Island.

'Absolutely,' replied Cici, her dark eyes sparkling. 'Mum brought me some totally divine presents. Like these.'

Cici slipped her feet into a pair of mega-fluffy white slippers that were tucked beside her bed. *Let's hope Summer never catches sight of those,* I thought to myself. *She would be in heaven!*

'That fur *is* fake, isn't it, Cici?' asked Meg.

'Yep! Totally fake,' Cici promised, her hand on her heart. 'Definitely no kittens or puppies were harmed in the making of my slippers.'

She tap-danced her way over to the wardrobe and flung open the door.

'And for heavenly beach days – this!' announced Cici, pulling a floaty white sundress off a hanger.

Cici held it up against her body and twirled around, her dead-straight, black hair fanning out. The dress had thin shoestring straps, lace trim and two strips of orange and blue flowers embroidered down the centre, from neckline to hem.

'That's adorable,' said Charlie. 'I love the embroidery.'

'It goes with my nails,' said Cici, placing her orange-tipped fingers against the matching flowers.

'White looks great on you,' added Meg. 'I always seem to get white things filthy.'

For some reason, the sight of Cici prancing around her perfect bedroom in her fluffy slippers and new dress suddenly made me feel extremely envious.

Doesn't Cici already have a perfectly gorgeous white dress? I asked myself.

Cici lay the dress out on the bed and went back to her wardrobe. 'That's not all – Mum bought me a divine cossie from a young up-and-coming Sydney designer.'

She pulled a bikini out of her top drawer. It was hot-pink and dotted with tiny yellow pineapples, spiked with green.

'Isn't it cute?' gushed Cici, holding it up for us to admire. 'The pineapples are so quirky. I love it.'

Super-duper cute, I agreed to myself. *But why couldn't I have a super-duper cute new cossie?* I thought of my own one-piece swimming costume – navy, boring and so old it was practically thin in patches. It had been my school swimming costume back in London and I hated it.

'Love the colours,' agreed Charlie.

Cici grinned with delight and put the swimming costume next to the dress on the bed. 'And she brought me these fantastic fabric paint pens that you can use to decorate material.' She fetched a stack of markers from her desk and fanned them out into a rainbow.

'What are you going to decorate?' asked Meg.

'I thought I'd get some plain white T-shirts and paint them with love hearts or write slogans on them,' explained Cici. She used her fingers to make quotation marks in the air. "Don't mess with me. I'm a fashionista",' she said in a mock tough voice.

Meg and Charlie laughed at her joke.

Cici suddenly noticed that I'd been rather quiet. 'What do you think, Pippa? Do you like them?'

I smiled tightly, trying not to look like I was positively green with envy.

'Of course, I love them, Cici,' I replied. 'You have the best wardrobe on the planet.'

'She certainly does,' agreed Meg.

Cici laughed. 'Thanks, guys. Why don't we go and watch a movie and have something to eat? Dad made some extra prawn-and-pork dumplings for us.'

So we went out the back to the living room and watched a movie, snacking on delicate dumplings with soy sauce and ginger. The movie was funny and cheered me up, so for a while I forgot all about Cici's new clothes and my total lack of any.

Afterwards, when we left to go home, Charlie climbed onto her beautiful bike.

'Do you want to double, Pippa?' she asked. 'I can give you a lift back to your place?'

I felt another stab of envy.

'No thanks, Charlie,' I said, shaking my head. 'That's okay. I can walk.'

'See you at school tomorrow,' said Meg.

My two friends rode off while Cici waved from the terrace. I trudged along home, walking into the wind with my head down. *What was wrong with me today? Why did I have this searing jealousy churning in my stomach? Why couldn't I just be happy for my friends?*

CHAPTER 2

BOO-BOO AND ZA-ZA

Thankfully, by Monday morning my bad mood had evaporated, helped along by an unexpected treat. Normally on school days we had breakfast with Mimi and Papa in their cottage. But today they were playing golf early, so we'd come to work with Mum. We all loved sampling the Beach Shack menu. Today the breakfast special was leek and mushroom frittata, which we'd polished off with a frothy Mango Madness smoothie.

The cafe was already busy. The air was filled with the delicious scent of ground coffee, cinnamon and toasting banana bread. A team of cyclists was sitting out on the jetty, wearing tight fluorescent lycra suits and drinking kale-and-celery smoothies. They were enthusiastically discussing kilometres, speeds and gradients.

Another group was crowded around the long refectory table, wearing gym clothes and chatting about downward dogs, cobras, crows and warriors. It was a little confusing until I realised they were talking about yoga poses.

Harry and I had just cleared away our breakfast plates and stacked them in the dishwasher when an older man shuffled in with his two fluffy Pomeranian dogs. One was brown, one was white, and they were both extremely yappy. I nudged Harry and giggled. Each dog wore a harness that was made to look like human clothes. The brown one wore a navy-and-white striped sailor suit, while the white dog wore a hot-pink frilly dress. Harry smothered a guffaw.

'Those dogs look ridiculous,' I whispered.

'I wonder why he dresses them up?' asked Harry. 'Maybe he thinks they're his children.'

'No one would dress a child like that,' I joked back. 'They'd refuse to go out in public.'

Our barista Zoe was making coffee at the espresso machine. Mum was out the front talking to Jason the builder. She'd asked me to help Zoe while she was gone.

'Good morning, Mr Jankowski,' called Zoe, as the old man headed out to the jetty with his dogs. 'Would you like your usual today?'

The old man grumbled something as he shambled past. The dogs yapped.

Zoe poured some steamed milk into a cup, making a delicate fern leaf pattern in the froth. She popped a slice of toasted banana bread on a plate, then two slices of cold fried bacon on another plate. The bacon was congealed and greasy. It looked disgusting.

'Pippa, could you please take this out to Mr Jankowski?' she asked. 'I still have to make all the coffees for the yoga class.'

'Is that his usual?' I asked. 'Banana bread and cold, greasy bacon? Yuck!'

Zoe grinned as she added a pat of butter beside the banana bread. 'The coffee and banana bread are for Mr Jankowski. The bacon is for his dogs, Boo-Boo and Za-Za.'

'*Boo-Boo* and *Za-Za*?' I demanded. 'Seriously?'

Zoe loaded the dishes onto a tray. 'Yes, Boo-boo's brown and Za-Za's white – easy to remember.'

'How did you have his order nearly ready before he even walked in the door?' I asked. 'What if he decided to have frittata this morning? Or he was late?'

Zoe laughed. 'Mr Jankowski comes in every morning at eight o'clock precisely and orders exactly the same thing. You could set your watch by him. In all the months I've been working here he's never changed his order.'

I pulled a face as I picked up the tray. 'That sounds super-boring. I'd hate to have exactly the same breakfast every day, at exactly the same time for months on end.'

'Some people like routine,' Zoe answered. 'It makes them feel better.'

I carried the tray onto the jetty and past the cyclists to where Mr Jankowski was sitting by himself, staring intently out to sea. Boo-Boo and Za-Za yapped noisily at me from under his chair. Mr Jankowski didn't take any notice.

'Hello, Mr Jankowski,' I said cheerily. 'Here's your coffee and banana bread.'

Mr Jankowski kept staring at the horizon. This was unusual. Most customers were friendly and chatty when I talked to them. Mrs Beecham always said our warm, welcoming atmosphere was what she enjoyed most about coming to the Beach Shack Cafe.

'And the bacon for the dogs,' I tried again in a slightly louder voice. 'I hope they enjoy it.'

Mr Jankowski bent down and patted Boo-Boo on the head (or was it Za-Za?), muttering something unintelligible under his breath.

I put the plates on the table in front of him, together with the cup of coffee, and flounced back to the kitchen with the tray.

'That Mr Jankowski is pretty grumpy,' I announced to Zoe. 'He wouldn't even talk to me.'

'He's lovely once you get to know him,' said Zoe. 'He's just very solitary.'

'Humph,' I huffed. 'Rude is more like it.'

Zoe picked up a tray of cappuccinos and lattes. 'I'm taking this to the yoga table.' She indicated another couple of cups. 'Would you mind taking those two out the front to Jason and your mum, please, Pippa? That's the last delivery for now.'

'Sure,' I said. I walked slowly, careful not to spill any of the coffee.

Mum was standing out the front of the cafe by the road, talking to Jason. Beside them was Jason's giant silvery-grey Great Dane called Hercules. A stack of shabby timber doors was piled in the back of the ute, painted pale-pink, purple and bright orange. One was covered in a huge luminous sticker saying 'When life shuts a door in your face, open another one. That's what doors are for.' I scoffed with derision. Who puts that on their door?

'They were really cheap, so I grabbed them,' said Jason, running his hand over the peeling paintwork as though they were masterpieces.

Mum winced at the garish colours. 'I can see why!'

'We can sand them back and once they're

painted white they'll be as good as new,' Jason assured her.

Mum frowned. 'Well, if you're certain they'll be okay . . .'

Jason grinned. 'The timber's solid and they were a fraction of the price of new ones. I saved you a fortune.'

Hercules saw me coming and woofed loudly in welcome, his tail thumping madly on the footpath.

'Here's our coffee delivery,' said Jason. 'Thanks so much, Pippa.'

Hercules lunged forward to nudge me, his snout right at tray height. I jerked back, making the coffee slop over the sides and into the saucers.

'Hercules, *no*,' I scolded. 'You made me spill them.'

Mum quickly rescued the cups, passing one to Jason and then taking one herself. 'Never mind, Pipkin,' she said. 'We didn't lose much.'

'Sorry, Pippa,' said Jason, pulling Hercules back by his lead and making him sit again. 'Hercules is feeling a bit neglected. We worked all weekend so I haven't had time to give him a good run.'

I stroked Hercules' velvety fur. He is the most gentle, affectionate dog but he's absolutely huge. He leaned against my side and rubbed his massive head against me like a kitten. Jason sometimes brings Hercules to work with him and he is usually beautifully behaved. He and Summer have become great friends.

Hercules looked up at me adoringly with his big grey eyes. It was as if he was begging me for some love and attention.

'I could take him for a walk,' I offered. 'I've finished helping Zoe and we don't have to be at school for another hour.'

Hercules jumped up, his tail wagging as if to say 'yes, please!'.

Jason grinned. 'He definitely knows the

32

meaning of W.A.L.K.' Jason spelled out the letters. Hercules pranced on all four paws.

'He can even spell it,' joked Mum. 'He's a clever dog.'

Jason glanced at me, then at Mum. 'Well, if it's okay with your mum, I'd love you to take Hercules for a little walk.'

Mum nodded. 'You've been working so hard on finishing the apartment, Jason, I feel like it's our fault you haven't had time to walk Hercules.'

'It's only a few more days of work,' said Jason. 'Then Hercules and I will be back to our usual routine of running on the beach every afternoon.'

I took Hercules by the lead. 'Harry can take Summer and we'll walk them together.'

Summer was super-excited at the prospect of an unexpected walk and Harry was happy to come along. When Mum was at work, Summer and Smudge usually stayed at home with Mimi and Papa, but recently Mum had been bringing Summer along to the cafe so she could get used to all the people coming and going.

The four of us set off along the esplanade that curved beside the cove.

Harry was telling me about one of the boys at school who had an enormous collection of crystals from all over the world. He sounded very enthusiastic about them, which is unusual for my brother, who's generally fairly quiet.

'Tom has this big rock that just looks like an ordinary dirty grey rock on the outside, but when you split it open, inside it's an amethyst crystal cave with heaps of miniature purple stalagmites and stalactites,' Harry said. 'It's called a geode and it's *soooo* cool.'

'It sounds amazing,' I said. 'Maybe you should collect crystals too.'

Harry pulled a disappointed face. 'You can buy them at the weekend markets but the special ones are pretty expensive.'

Hercules loped along with Summer trotting close behind him. The two dogs sniffed at interesting scents and said hello to other dogs being walked in the sunshine.

A huge flock of seagulls wheeled and screeched above the beach, their wings like white sails. A man cycled by, towing a trailer that was laden high with groceries. On the grass were three fire jugglers practising with firesticks. They had dreadlocked hair and wore tie-dyed T-shirts. Another one was tightrope walking on a thick rope tied between two palm trees. It was like a mini circus.

We were just about to turn around and head back to the cafe when I noticed a fluffy black puppy tearing towards us. He was being chased by a woman pushing a pram and shouting. The woman looked like she had a whole watermelon tucked under her shirt, but then I realised she must be expecting a baby.

'Look,' I said to Harry. 'It's a runaway puppy.'

'Rufus. Rufus! Come here, you naughty boy!' yelled his owner.

A businessman in a suit tried to grab the puppy, but the runaway twisted and sidestepped and kept racing towards us.

'Rufus. STOP!' shouted his owner, sounding frantic.

As he came closer, I noticed the puppy was trailing a long red lead. A jogger tried to grab it, but the puppy was too quick. Summer whined and pulled, keen to join in the game of puppy chasing. Harry held her firmly.

Suddenly, Rufus noticed Hercules and Summer and hurtled towards us. He skidded to a stop at our feet and rolled onto his back, all four paws in the air. Summer licked him all over the face. I grabbed him by the collar and held him tight.

The woman stopped running and hobbled towards us. She was panting hard from her exertion. The dark-haired toddler in the pram looked like he had enjoyed every second of the excitement.

'Again, Mama, again,' he insisted, waving his arms in the air with delight.

'No way, Carlo,' she said to him. 'I can hardly walk, let alone run.'

She stopped the pram when she reached us, still puffing.

'Thank you *so* much for catching Rufus,' the mother said. 'As you can see, it's a little hard for me to run at the moment.'

'That's okay,' I said, bending down and ruffling the pup's curly black ears. 'He's adorable.'

'He's adorably wicked,' she said ruefully, taking the lead from me. 'Carlo threw his hat out of the pram and when I reached down to pick it up, Rufus's lead slipped out of my hand and he took off like a rocket. I thought he was going to run onto the road and be hit by a car.'

'Luckily, he wanted to say hello to our dogs so he was easy to grab,' I replied. 'Our puppy, Summer, is just the same.'

'Aren't your two dogs beautiful?' she said. 'I love your Great Dane. He's magnificent.'

Hercules lifted his nose proudly, as though to say 'of course I am'.

'Hercules isn't ours,' I corrected her. 'He belongs to our builder. We're just taking him for a quick walk while he's at work.'

'Oh, you do dog walking?' she asked. 'I've been looking for someone to help exercise Rufus for me. It can be tricky walking him when I get so busy with Carlo, and it will be even harder in a few days when the new baby comes.'

'No, I don't,' I said. 'We usually just take it in turns to walk Summer after school. It's the first time I've walked Hercules.'

'Oh, that's a pity,' said the woman. 'Thanks again for rescuing Rufus.'

She said goodbye and headed off, dragging

a reluctant Rufus behind her. By this stage, Harry and I were in danger of being late for school so we raced back to the cafe, the two dogs galloping along beside us.

We had just arrived back at the cafe when Hercules screeched to a complete stop, almost sitting down on his haunches. He was trembling with terror. He leapt behind my legs and tried to hide, which, considering how huge he was, was never going to work. I stroked Hercules' silvery back and looked around, wondering what on earth could have upset him. Then I realised that Hercules was absolutely petrified of ... Boo-Boo and Za-Za!

Mr Jankowski was hobbling out the front door of the cafe, being led by the two tiny Pomeranians. They caught sight of Summer and Hercules and started to yap in high-pitched, ferocious voices. Summer rolled onto her back in a totally submissive position, displaying her tummy for a rub. But Hercules was curled up into the smallest possible space (which was still enormous) with his eyes shut as though that might make him invisible. I couldn't believe it! When Hercules couldn't take it anymore, he turned and ran, dragging me behind him.

'Stop, Hercules,' I yelled, pulling hard on the lead with all my might.

Za-Za and Boo-Boo gave chase. Poor Mr Jankowski was yanked forward. He tripped over the uneven footpath and went flying. I stopped Hercules and dragged him back behind me, giving the lead to Harry.

'Take Hercules to Jason and ask Mum to come here,' I ordered. 'Mr Jankowski might be hurt.'

I crouched next to Mr Jankowski, who was sprawled on the footpath, tangled in the leads and yapping dogs. I pulled the two dogs away from him by their collars.

'Are you all right, Mr Jankowski?' I asked. 'Have you hurt yourself?'

'I'll be all right in a minute,' he muttered. But he looked very pale and shaken.

Mum and Zoe arrived at the same time. Zoe, who is a volunteer surf lifesaver, calmly and methodically checked over Mr Jankowski. I held the two dogs by their leads away from their owner before they licked him to pieces.

'Does it hurt here?' asked Zoe, gently touching one of his legs. 'What about here?'

'Should I call an ambulance?' asked Mum, looking worried.

'No, I'm fine,' said Mr Jankowski gruffly. 'Just help me to my feet and I'll walk home.'

Mum and Zoe helped him up, but we could all see he wasn't quite as fine as he claimed. His ankle looked puffy and swollen. Mr Jankowski planted his foot on the ground to take weight on it but winced with pain.

'I think it could be a sprained ankle, Mr Jankowski,' said Zoe, examining the swelling.

'You need to elevate it and ice it for a while to reduce the inflammation.'

'Nonsense,' said Mr Jankowski. 'I'll be perfectly fine. Just call me a taxi.'

'I can run you home myself in a little while,' said Mum. 'But first let's get you settled inside with an icepack.'

Mum and Zoe helped Mr Jankowski into the cafe and sat him down in a comfortable chair. I hovered around, holding the two dogs and watching. Zoe elevated Mr Jankowski's leg and strapped an icepack to his ankle while Mum fetched a cushion to make his foot more comfortable. Suddenly she checked the time.

'Goodness, Pipkin, it's after nine o'clock,' Mum cried. 'You kids are going to be so late!'

I shoved Boo-Boo and Za-Za's leads into Mum's hand, then Harry, Bella and I ran all the way to school, our backpacks bumping up and down on our backs.

CHAPTER 3

BEACH BLUES

The school day was the usual mix of maths, English, art and playtime. The highlight was after recess when we had our first round of speeches. Mrs Marshall picked one student at a time to give a prepared, one-minute talk that we'd worked on in class the week before. We all had to give a speech about something we were truly passionate about.

The topics were varied and interesting, from Rory talking about how homework should be banned to Tash speaking about how hard she was working to try out for the State Gymnastics Championships. Alex told us about the importance of sustainable farming and encouraging people to eat locally grown food, while Olivia spoke eloquently about how vital it is for children in developing countries to have access to education and how literacy could help break the poverty cycle.

The speeches were all really good. I hoped Mrs Marshall wouldn't call me up next because I suddenly felt that my prepared speech on how much I loved designing and drawing wasn't quite up to scratch.

After school, the Sassy Sisters had organised to head to the cove near the Beach Shack Cafe for a swim. We walked down the cobbled main piazza, past the colourful shops and restaurants, while we chatted about our day. Bella raced on ahead with Charlie's sister Daisy while Harry lagged behind with his friend Tom, examining a fistful of different crystals.

As we passed the surf shop, a huge sign caught my eye.

SALE!
30% off swimwear
Ends Saturday

In the window were three mannequins wearing different swimming costumes. One was khaki, another was aqua with pale-pink roses and green leaves, and the third was a bold floral pattern of cobalt-blue and white. They were all gorgeous.

'So, Pippa, which do you think was the best?' asked Charlie.

'S-sorry . . . um . . .' I stammered, my mind snapping back to the conversation. 'Maybe the blue-and-white one?'

The girls all roared with laughter.

'Weren't you listening, Pippa?' asked Charlie. 'I meant everyone's speeches today. Who did a better job? Olivia or Alex?'

'Oh,' I said, feeling embarrassed. 'Olivia, definitely.'

'I thought so too,' agreed Meg. 'She's a great speaker.'

'I thought you might say Alex,' said Cici, with a sly grin. 'You were just looking very daydream-y.'

I flushed. 'No, I was checking out the swimming costumes in the window.'

The girls all swung back around to look at them.

Cici nodded knowingly. 'Oh, definitely the blue-and-white. That would look *adorable* on you. And they're on sale.'

'Only this week,' I said longingly. Where would I get the money for a swimming costume in the next few days?

'I love the one with the pink roses,' said Charlie. 'It's so pretty.'

I took another long look at the swimming costumes. A smaller sign under the cobalt swimming costume read.

~~$90~~ **reduced to $60**

I had visions of how lovely it would feel to wear a really pretty costume to the beach instead of my despised old one. I imagined taking my old costume and tossing it in the garbage bin. That would feel amazing.

We all trooped into the cafe and said hello to Mum, who was sitting at one of the small tables with a calculator and a pile of invoices.

'Good news, Pippa,' said Mum, giving me a hug. 'I've just got off the phone from the storage warehouse. All our boxes are getting delivered first thing Thursday morning.'

'Yay!' I gave a little skip of excitement. Most of our belongings had been in storage for months. We'd sold or given away lots of our furniture and knick-knacks. It was too hard to ship them halfway across the world. We'd each brought a suitcase with our favourite clothes, a few toys and books. Everything else had been packed away in boxes. There was definitely no room in the caravan for extra stuff.

'That's so exciting, Pippa,' said Meg. 'It will be like Christmas discovering all your old treasures.'

'I can't wait to unpack my books and put them on the shelf,' I said. 'And my art supplies.'

Mum stood up, shuffling all the papers together in a pile.

'Do you girls want some afternoon tea here?' she asked. 'Or would you like to take a picnic to the beach?'

I looked around at the other girls. 'Picnic on the beach?'

'Great idea,' said Charlie.

I helped Mum put together a picnic basket with containers of chopped watermelon, mango and pineapple while the girls changed out of their school uniforms.

Then I pulled on my swimming costume, grabbed my towel and raced to meet the others.

'Thanks, Mum,' I said, as I scooped up the picnic basket on my way out the door.

Down on the beach we dropped our towels, hats and the picnic basket on the coral-white sand. This part of the cove was calm and pro-tected, with small foaming waves where it is usually safe to swim. Further out, colourful fishing boats bobbed up and down on their moorings. Palm trees fringed the shore.

A group of parents were building an elab-orate sandcastle with their children. A cute toddler charged up the beach wearing a yellow-and-black bumblebee swimming costume with tiny black wings on her back.

'Race you in,' cried Cici, as she tore down the beach. The other girls gave chase, Meg slowly gaining on her.

'Not fair,' called Charlie, slowing to a walk. 'You had a head start.'

'Snoozers are losers,' yelled Cici, as she splashed into the shallows. The girls began chasing each other, squealing at the shock of the cool water. Droplets of water sparkled in the sun. I wished I had Mum's camera as I watched the girls ducking and prancing in their bright costumes against the brilliant turquoise of the cove.

Cici was wearing her new pineapple bikini, which looked gorgeous with her dark hair and skin. Charlie was wearing a flamboyant floral design and had her blonde hair loose, long and wavy down her back. Meg's costume was a spotty blue one-piece with spaghetti straps – practical for running, swimming and surfing.

The girls in their pretty swimming costumes made my old school swimmers look even more tatty than usual. I crossed my arms, feeling sorry for myself all over again.

'Come on, Pippa,' called Charlie. 'The water's heavenly.'

'Coming,' I replied, giving myself a firm mental shake. Next I'd be jealous of the toddler in her bumblebee swimsuit!

I ran as fast as I could down the beach and dived into the water. I swam out strongly, trying to burn up some of my cranky energy.

After our swim, we sat on the sand and chomped on some icy cold watermelon while we chatted about our plans for the weekend.

'I had a brilliant idea,' said Charlie. 'On Saturday, we could pack a picnic lunch and cycle over to Secret Cove on the other side of the island. It's so quiet and secluded there.'

'That would be fun,' said Meg. 'We could take our masks and flippers and snorkel over the coral. We should see lots of beautiful fish there.'

'I'm in,' said Cici. 'I can make some mini cheesy muffins for lunch.'

'How about you, Pippa?' asked Charlie. 'Maybe your mum could make us something yummy for lunch too?'

My cranky mood flared up again. 'It sounds great, Charlie. But have you forgotten? I don't actually have a bike.'

Meg put her hand on my arm. 'You can always borrow my brother's bike. Jack won't mind.'

Charlie looked miffed at my snarky response.

'You don't *have* to come, Pippa,' she said. 'You don't have to be so grumpy either.'

I immediately felt remorseful. 'Sorry, Charlie. The bike ride sounds fantastic, but all our stuff is getting delivered this week so I need to help Mum with unpacking.'

'That's *soooo* exciting, Pippa,' said Cici. 'Do you want us to come and help you?'

'No,' I replied. 'That's okay. You guys go for the picnic. I'll be fine.'

The girls chattered on about what they

would see and do at Secret Cove. I wondered what I might have packed in those boxes . . . Perhaps, by some miracle, I had some lovely new clothes in there just waiting to be rediscovered.

The girls cycled off home and I went back inside the cafe. I still had this hollow feeling in my chest. The cafe was empty as it was nearly closing time. Zoe was sitting at the long table, looking at her computer, surrounded by books and papers. I dumped the picnic basket on the kitchen bench and wandered over to her.

Zoe looked up and smiled. 'Hi, Pippa. Did you have a nice swim?'

I shrugged, my mouth turned down at the corners. 'It was all right. Where's Mum?' I asked, changing the subject.

'Your mum's upstairs checking the tiling in the bathroom with Jason,' said Zoe.

I sat down at the table next to her, wondering what she was doing. It was usually Mum who did all the accounting and finances.

But the papers weren't cafe receipts or bills as I'd first thought. There was a fat handbook, marked with yellow sticky notes and lots of loose pieces of paper covered in handwritten scrawls.

'What's all this stuff?' I asked curiously.

Zoe looked up at me with sparkling green eyes and an air of suppressed excitement.

'I'm doing my application for uni,' she announced. 'It's due tomorrow.'

'Uni?' I asked in horror. 'What do you mean you're doing a uni application?'

Zoe laughed at my shocked face. 'I'm applying to study physiotherapy. It's *really* hard to get into, but I'm hoping that with my school marks and my surf lifesaving volunteer work I'll get in next year.'

My stomach plummeted with disappointment. A tiny part of me wished that Zoe wouldn't get into university, then she'd stay with us forever.

'But I thought you liked being a barista here at the cafe,' I said. 'I thought you liked living on Kira Island?'

'I love working at the Beach Shack Cafe,' Zoe assured me. 'I love living on Kira Island. But my plan was always to work here for a year and save up as much money as I could so I can afford to go to university.'

'Oh,' I said, feeling even sorrier for myself. I loved having Zoe working at the cafe. She was much more than just an employee. She was a real friend.

I felt a hard lump in my throat. This day seemed to be going from bad to worse. I blinked rapidly.

'Don't worry, Pippa,' Zoe said sympatheti-cally. 'I won't be going for a few months yet.'

'Oh, that's good,' I lied, my shoulders hunched. I couldn't stop the feeling that nothing in my life was going the way I wanted it to today.

'Is there something else worrying you, Pippa?' asked Zoe, with concern. 'You seem a bit down this afternoon?'

That's an understatement, I thought.

'I'm really sad you'll be going away, although I *am* happy you'll be doing something you've always wanted to do . . .'

I hesitated, not sure if I wanted to tell her what was upsetting me, but Zoe's manner was so warm and understanding that I decided to share my woes. I hoped she didn't think I was a completely selfish brat.

'It's just hard sometimes,' I said. 'The girls are planning a bike ride to Secret Cove on the weekend, but I don't have a bike. Then Cici's mum came back from her trip and brought Cici all these totally amazing presents.'

'Cici's mum has been away for work for two weeks,' Zoe reminded me. 'Of course she's going to bring her some totally amazing presents.'

'I know, but we never have any money and all my friends seem to have lots of things I don't have,' I said. 'Like beautiful bedrooms, heaps of cool clothes and pretty swimming costumes that aren't old and saggy . . . I shouldn't moan, but there's a lovely cossie on sale at the surf shop this week and I just wish I had the money to buy it.'

I blinked back tears. Zoe gave me a hug. I knew she'd understand. Then she pushed me away and looked me sternly in the face.

'Philippa Hamilton,' said Zoe. 'Are you feeling jealous of your lovely friends and their belongings?'

I sniffed, feeling ashamed of myself, then nodded.

'Don't you know you are one of the luckiest girls on the planet?' Zoe asked. 'Living on this beautiful island with a family that adores you and great friends who look out for you?'

'I know,' I said, sniffing again.

Zoe thought for a moment, fiddling with one of her silver hoop earrings. 'Jealousy is a horrible thing. It eats you up so you can't see the good things in your life. I know because I've been there too.'

'What do you mean?' I asked.

'When I finished school last year, I really wanted to go to university, but I come from a big family and money is always *really* tight,' Zoe explained.

'I know that feeling,' I said, with a rueful smile.

'Some of my friends came from wealthier families and their parents could afford to send them away to university and pay for everything,' Zoe continued. 'But as much as my parents love me and want the very best for me, they just couldn't afford that.'

Zoe pushed a red curl behind one ear. 'All my friends were talking about the courses they were going to do and the clubs they were going to join, which drove me mad with envy. At first I was furious with the world and my parents, and that made me utterly miserable. I was horrible to live with!'

'I can't imagine you ever being horrible to live with,' I replied.

'Jealousy can make even the loveliest people all bitter and nasty,' said Zoe. 'Anyway, Mum suggested that rather than being jealous of my friends, I could change my thoughts to be more positive. I could use my envy to *help* me achieve my dreams – to give me the incentive I needed to work hard and save money so I could afford to go to uni too.'

I nodded. 'That makes sense.'

Zoe smiled at me. 'I decided to go away for a year, work super-hard and save all my money so I could achieve my dream myself. That's why I came to Kira Island, and wasn't that the *best* decision ever?'

Zoe's explanation completely changed how

I was feeling. Suddenly I wanted Zoe to achieve her dream of studying physiotherapy more than anything. I gave her a big hug. 'I'm so glad you did, or I'd never have met you. I'm really happy you'll be going to uni next year, but please promise me you'll come back and visit sometimes.'

'Of course I will,' Zoe said. 'Your mum's already said I can come back and work in the summer holidays.'

'Yay,' I said. 'The Beach Shack just won't be the same without you.'

'I've loved my time here,' Zoe said. 'You're like my second family. And I'm *really* going to miss everyone, but especially you, Pippa.'

Zoe packed up her things. 'Now that dishwasher is finally finished, so I'd better empty it.'

'Thanks, Zoe,' I said. 'I feel so much better after talking to you.'

I put the picnic basket away, thinking about

everything Zoe had said. How could I use my own feelings of envy in a more positive way? How could I get inspired to make my own dreams come true?

CHAPTER 4

MY BRILLIANT PLAN

As usual, my brilliant idea came in the middle of the night. All I needed to do was to work hard and make some money, just like Zoe had. Of course, I had school during the day and lots to do to help Mum, but I suddenly thought of a solution to my problems.

I was going to start my own business. And Rufus the runaway puppy had given me the perfect plan.

First, I asked Mum if it was okay. She was

a little reluctant at first, but when I begged and begged she said I could trial it for a couple of weeks to make sure it didn't affect my homework or my chores. I couldn't wait to tell the girls about it at school.

The first lesson on Tuesday morning was art. It was one of my favourite classes, especially as the art teacher, Miss Annand, is happy to let us chat and laugh while we work. She plays soft music in the background and never ever gets cross. The art room is delightful chaos, with colourful paintings on the wall, shelves stacked with books and the smell of dried clay and turpentine.

Charlie, Cici, Meg and I were sitting around a paint-splattered table, perched on stools and poring over our sketches.

Everyone in the class was creating individual birds, which would later be glued onto a tree we'd painted on a huge canvas.

I was sketching a superb fairy-wren, copying from a photograph in a bird book. Cici was painting a cheeky sulphur-crested cockatoo with outstretched wings and Charlie was drawing a powerful owl with round orange eyes. Meg was copying a chubby little penguin to sit beside the burrow at the base of the tree.

'Your wren is so delicate,' said Meg. 'My penguin is looking extremely lopsided.'

'You just need to take a little width off his tummy there,' I suggested, pointing with my paintbrush. Meg rubbed out the line where I'd suggested and tried again.

I compared the different blues from the tubes of paint available, trying to match the colour of the photo.

The cobalt-blue reminded me of the pretty swimming costume I'd spied in the surf shop window. The swimming costume that was now on sale and that I so desperately wanted. I squeezed out a big blob of colour and swirled it around with my paintbrush.

'I've had an idea,' I said, 'to make some extra pocket money.'

'Don't you earn pocket money by helping your mum at the cafe?' Charlie asked.

'I did,' I said, 'but Harry, Bella and I decided we wouldn't take any money from Mum until the apartment was finished. Plus, we promised we'd help pay for Summer and Smudge's vet bills. We thought it might help get the building finished *heaps* faster if Mum didn't have to pay us pocket money!'

We all giggled because of course I knew that our tiny sum of pocket money was not enough to get the apartment built any quicker.

'So why do you want to make extra money?' asked Meg.

I hesitated, not sure if I wanted to admit to the other girls how I'd been feeling jealous. Then I decided it was best to be honest.

'As you all know,' I announced. 'I *hate* my horrible, saggy, daggy swimming costume.

And I'm desperate to buy a new one, especially as they're on sale.'

'Yours is rather shabby,' Cici agreed, as she tinted the cockatoo's crest a vibrant yellow. 'You're long overdue for a more tropical makeover.'

I nodded in agreement. 'Not only that, but I'd really like to save up for a new bike so I can go cycling with you guys around the island.'

Charlie raised her eyebrows. 'So you're talking some serious pocket money. How are you going to do that?'

I took a deep breath, my heart skipping with excitement. 'I'm going to start a business.'

The other girls stopped painting and looked at me with astonishment.

'A business?' asked Charlie. 'What sort of business?'

'A dog-walking business,' I said. 'I think there'd be lots of people, like Mr Jankowski or Jason the builder, who'd be happy to pay me to walk their dogs.'

I looked at the other girls. No one said anything. Maybe they thought it was a really stupid idea.

'I could do other things too,' I faltered. 'Like dog washing and grooming and picking up poo.'

Meg squeezed my arm to reassure me. 'That sounds like a really clever way of making money.'

Charlie nodded. 'There are so many people with dogs on Kira Island. I'm sure lots of them would like some extra help, especially with picking up poo!'

Charlie should know. With two dogs, two donkeys, some chickens, a cat and a pet lamb, her family was always cleaning up after their animals.

Cici grinned at me. 'You'll need a brilliant name for your business. Something that rhymes or has alliteration to make it sound memorable.' She thought for a moment then put on a mega-dramatic voice. 'Like "Awesome Pawsome", or "Woofy Walkers"!'

Charlie giggled. 'How about "Furbaby Funtime"?'

'Or "Poochy Paws"?' added Meg.

'I like "The Sassy Strollers",' I said, getting into the fun.

Cici mimed strutting in a super-sassy fashion, with her nose in the air, one hand on her hip and the other stretched out as though she was being led along by a posh poodle. We all chuckled. Cici is definitely going to end up on the stage one day.

'"Posh Puppies",' suggested Charlie. 'Or "Precocious Pooches"? Or "Posh Precocious Poochy Puppies"!'

We laughed so loudly that Miss Annand glanced over to check on us. We quickly bent our heads over our drawings and worked like mad.

'Choosing a name is *sooo* hard,' I moaned, as

I coloured in the fairy-wren's blue cheeks and tail. 'I want people to take me seriously. They won't trust me with their precious puppies if they think I'm silly.'

'How about "Pippa's Perfect Pooch Pampering"?' said Meg.

I tested it, rolling the words around on my tongue.

'Brilliant,' said Cici. 'That's the one.'

Meg glowed at Cici's praise.

'So now you just need to make a plan,' said Charlie. 'Work out how you're going to advertise the business and find customers.'

'Mum wrote a business plan when she bought the boathouse,' I said. 'She said it helped her work out what her objectives were going to be.'

'We can all help,' said Cici. 'Four heads are better than one!'

I pushed my half-finished fairy-wren to the side, pulled out my notebook from my pile of books and turned to a fresh page.

We brainstormed ideas and I wrote the best ones down. This is what we came up with:

Business Plan for Pippa's Perfect Pooch Pampering

My mission: pet services with a smile and lots of puppy pampering including dog walking, bathing, grooming, pooper-scoopering, cuddles, pats and playing ball.

To do:

1) Create advertising to find customers - posters, ad in the local paper, story in the school newspaper?

2) Write copy for advertising poster including services and phone number. (Ask Mum if I can use the Beach Shack Cafe's number? Could choose a set time to take bookings like 5 pm, just after closing.)

3) Meg to take a photo of me for the poster.

4) Charlie to design posters on the computer.

5) Print posters.

6) Visit shops and businesses and ask if they will display posters. Could try cafe, vet hospital, pet shop, deli, supermarket and school noticeboard.

7) Wait by the phone for the customers to call.

8) Save up enough money to buy a new swimming costume and bike!

I didn't get my fairy-wren painting finished, but by the time the bell went after class, I had a good plan to start my pooch pampering business.

All I needed to do was walk six dogs for one hour each this week and I would have my sixty dollars for a new swimming costume. In a few weeks, I might even have enough money to buy a vintage-style bike with a wicker basket on the front, just like Charlie's. And in a few months I might have enough money to buy . . . well, who knows what I could buy? Crystals for Harry? Some new books for Bella? Maybe something really special for Mum?

After school, the four of us went to Meg's yacht to work on designing a poster. Meg borrowed her mum's camera and took some photos of me so we could choose the best one to put on the poster.

'A *big* smile, Pippa,' said Meg, checking the screen. 'Remember, your mission is to provide pet services with a smile.'

I gave an even bigger smile as Meg snapped the photo.

'That's perfect,' said Charlie.

'Now, what are you going to say in your ad?' asked Cici. 'I think the heading should be the name of your business.'

'You want to make sure you sound professional,' said Meg.

We tossed ideas around.

'Dog walking from 7.30 to 8.30 am and 3.30 to 6.30 pm?' I suggested.

'I don't think you should do it before school,' said Charlie. 'Perhaps you should start small and see how you go.'

'Why not say that you'll walk dogs after school from 3.30 to 4.30 and on weekends?' said Meg. 'Then you can add extra time if you need to.'

With the girls' help I came up with some ideas for my advertisement, jotting it all down on some scrap paper. I drafted one version and read it out loud.

'Mmm,' said Meg. 'It sounds professional but . . .'

'It's not quite right,' said Charlie, shaking her head.

'I don't want to be negative,' said Cici. 'But it's a bit boring. You want the ad to sound interesting and exciting, to reinforce how much fun the dogs are going to have. No one wants their pooch to be bored to death.'

I rewrote it, trying to make it more lively and friendly.

'How about this?' I asked. Then I read out my second draft.

Pippa's Perfect Pooch Pampering

Pippa Hamilton, 11, is an experienced dog walker with her own mischievous golden retriever puppy called Summer. Pippa is available to walk dogs after school from

3.30 to 4.30 pm and on weekends. Her friendly pooch pampering services include:

- Dog walking at Pelican Park (pick up from your home) with lots of playing ball, tug of war and pats – $10 per hour
- Dog grooming and bathing at your home with cuddles – $10
- Pooper-scoopering with a smile – cleaning up doggy mess in your garden – $5

Please phone the Beach Shack Cafe between 5 and 6 pm to make bookings.

'Much better,' said Cici. 'That sounds more like the sort of pampering I'd like Muffin to have.'

So I typed it up on Meg's mum's computer, then handed it over to Charlie, who is the best at graphic design. She added in the photo that Meg had taken and laid it out perfectly with a decorative border. Cici double-checked it to make sure there were no spelling mistakes and Meg printed off ten colour copies on the printer.

I felt a thrill of pride as I saw my professional-looking business poster.

'Now let's stick them up in all the right places,' said Cici.

The girls came with me as I set off, armed with Blu-Tack, to deliver my posters. The first couple we stuck up in our cafe, inside near the cash register and outside by the front door. Mum and Zoe were very impressed. I saved a couple to put up on the school noticeboards tomorrow.

Next we headed off to ask if we could stick up posters at the delicatessen, pet shop, supermarket, surf shop and greengrocer. All the shopkeepers were happy for me to put up my posters, although it took quite a while to explain to each one what it was all about.

Finally we went to the Kira Cove veterinary hospital, tucked away in the side street behind the main piazza.

Willow's mum, Caitlin, was the vet there and she had often looked after Summer and Smudge. Caitlin was standing behind the reception desk checking the computer screen when we arrived. The waiting room was filled with patients and their owners, sitting on chairs against the wall. There were cats and guinea pigs in carry cages, dogs of all sizes straining on their leads and even a baby goat with a hot-pink collar and harness.

Charlie gazed around in delight as she took in the assembled pets. She loved animals of all kinds and hoped to be a vet herself one day. With a wave, she went to say hello to the goat and her owner.

'Hello, girls,' Caitlin greeted us. 'I hope everything is all right with your beautiful pets?'

We all said hi in return.

'Everything's fine,' I said. 'We're not here about any of our animals. I was hoping I could put a poster up in your window, please?'

'What's it about?' asked Caitlin.

'I'm starting a dog-walking business after school and I thought some of your clients might have dogs they need walked or groomed,' I replied. 'I'm trying to earn some extra pocket money.'

Caitlin scanned the poster I held out to her.

'Absolutely, Pippa,' said Caitlin. 'That's a wonderful idea. I'm sure I have quite a few clients who need some extra help with their pets. Are you just looking after dogs, or will you take on other animals as well? I have a client who's going away and needs his diamond python looked after for a month.'

'A pet python?' asked Cici, with horror. 'That's disgusting.'

'A diamond python isn't dangerous,' protested Meg. 'They make fantastic pets.'

I shuddered at the thought. Our caravan was crowded enough with Mum, three children, one puppy and a kitten. We definitely didn't need a pet python in the mix.

'Just dogs to start with,' I said. 'And I'll see how it goes. I don't think Mum would like it much if I looked after any extra animals at home. Especially not *snakes*.'

Caitlin smiled at my reluctance. 'Balthazar is a lovely python, but I totally understand. Put the poster up in the window by the door and I'll spread the word.'

I used the Blu-Tack to stick the poster to the inside of the window. We said goodbye to Caitlin and headed off towards the beachfront, where we would all split up.

'Thanks so much for coming with me, guys,' I said to the others.

'Fingers crossed you get some customers,' said Meg.

'Good luck, Pippa,' added Charlie. 'Let me know if you need any help with it. I'd be happy to help you walk the dogs.'

I walked back to the cafe while the other girls headed to their own homes.

It was nearly five o'clock. I wondered if anyone would ring, wanting me to look after their dogs. I wondered if the dogs would be well-behaved. I felt a little flutter of butterfly wings in my tummy.

CHAPTER 5

MR JANKOWSKI

As I walked into the cafe, Mum was talking on the phone. It was five o'clock and the cafe was supposed to be closed. I hoped she wouldn't stay on the phone very long. What if one of my potential customers was trying to ring?

Mum put down the phone as I came up to the counter.

'Who was that?' I asked eagerly. 'Was it someone wanting me to walk their dog?'

Mum laughed and shook her head. 'Sorry,

Pipkin. No one's rung about your dog walking yet. That was just the furniture removalist organising our delivery.'

I huffed with disappointment.

'I hope someone rings soon,' I said. 'I need to get some customers fast.'

'Yes, that reminds me,' said Mum. 'I do have an idea for your first dog-walking customer.'

My heart thumped with excitement. 'Really? Who is it?'

'I thought you might be able to walk Hercules again this week,' said Mum. 'The builders are working late every day to get the apartment finished, so it would be a huge help for Jason. He might need you to walk him on the weekend too as they'll probably have to work then as well.'

'I'd love to,' I said, my mind immediately calculating how much money I would earn at ten dollars per walk. That would go a long way towards my new swimming costume.

'That's what I told Jason,' said Mum, beaming at me. 'And I also told him you wouldn't think of taking any money for it when he was working so hard to get the apartment ready for us.'

My heart plummeted. *No money . . . Not even a little bit?* I thought of everything that Jason was doing to help us move into our new home – working long hours, saving Mum money by searching for bargains and working on weekends. Of course I couldn't ask Jason for money.

'Sure, Mum,' I replied, trying my best not to sound disappointed. 'Of course I'll walk Hercules for Jason.'

'I thought perhaps you could walk Summer in the morning before school,' suggested Mum. 'And then you will have the afternoon free for Hercules and your clients.'

'Okay,' I agreed.

I hovered by the phone, hoping someone would ring with a booking for me. But for once the phone was completely silent. Mum shut down the cash register while Zoe put the last coffee cups away. Harry, Bella and Summer had already gone back home with Mimi and Papa, so I had to wait until Mum had finished for the day. Zoe said goodbye and left on her bicycle to ride to her apartment.

'Come on, Pipkin,' said Mum, the keys in her hand. 'It's time to finish up.'

I looked at the silent phone. 'Maybe we should wait just a little bit longer.'

'No one's going to ring now, Pipkin,' said Mum. 'It's way past closing time.'

I walked out to the car, feeling glum. There hadn't been one phone call for my new business. Not one person wanted me to walk their dogs. It was already Tuesday and the swimming costumes were only on sale until the end of the week. At this rate I'd never make the money.

Mum carried a basket to the car and placed it on the back seat.

'Sorry, Pipkin,' said Mum. 'I just need to drop this basket off on our way home.'

'Where are we going?' I asked as I fastened my seat belt.

'I packed up some leftovers for Mr Jankowski,' Mum said. 'He's not supposed to walk far for a few days with that sprained ankle and I thought he might appreciate some food.'

Mr Jankowski lived near the cafe, in one of the side streets that ran down towards Kira Cove. Mum pulled up in front of an old white-washed cottage. The front garden must once have been very pretty with its bougainvillea and frangipani, but it was now overgrown with knee-high weeds and grass.

I followed Mum up onto the front veranda. There was the sound of yapping from inside as she pressed the doorbell. We waited a few minutes, then Mum knocked on the door.

'Hello, Mr Jankowski,' she called. 'Are you there? It's Jenna Hamilton from the Beach Shack Cafe.'

There was a shuffling sound from inside and then the front door opened. Mr Jankowski was leaning on a crutch, his ankle bound in a bandage. Boo-Boo and Za-Za shot between his legs and jumped around us, yipping and barking. They weren't wearing their human clothes now, and with their thick fur I thought they looked exactly like Cici's fluffy new slippers, although, of course, one was brown.

'Thank you for driving me home yesterday, Jenna,' said Mr Jankowski. His voice sounded hoarse, as though he didn't use it very often. 'It was most considerate of you.'

'Not at all,' said Mum. 'It was a pleasure. Are you feeling better now?'

'It's a little better today.' He gestured at his sore ankle. 'Please give my compliments to your charming barista, Zoe, for looking after me. The doctor said she did a sterling job of bandaging me up.'

He glanced at me. 'And thanks to you too, young lady, for looking after my naughty dogs.'

'That's all right, Mr Jankowsi,' I replied.

Mum turned to me. 'This is my daughter Pippa.'

'Delighted to meet you, Miss Hamilton,' said Mr Jankowski.

Mum indicated the basket she carried over her arm. 'I brought you some quiche Lorraine and some banana bread for the morning, as well as a few other bits and pieces. I thought you might like some dinner that didn't need preparing.'

'You brought me food?' asked Mr Jankowski, his voice sounding even more croaky than before. 'That is so very kind of you.'

'It was left over from today,' said Mum. 'Can I carry it in for you? I don't want to keep you standing.'

Mr Jankowski looked embarrassed. 'It's a bit of a mess. I live alone. My wife . . . my wife died a few months ago.'

Mr Jankowski's face crumpled with grief.

'I'm so sorry to hear that,' said Mum gently. 'Why don't I pack these in the fridge for you?'

Mr Jankowski limped as he showed us the way to the kitchen at the back of the cottage. The kitchen was untidy with a pile of unwashed dishes in the sink, a dead plant on the windowsill and a messy pile of newspapers on the table.

Mum settled Mr Jankowski in a chair at the kitchen table, with his leg elevated on another chair. She gave him the warm quiche Lorraine on a plate with some salad, then chatted to him as she packed the rest of the food away in the virtually empty fridge. While Mum talked, I sat at the table and absentmindedly doodled some fairy-wrens in the margin of the newspaper with a pen that was lying there.

'Do the dogs need to be fed?' asked Mum. 'Perhaps Pippa can do that for you to save you getting up?'

Mr Jankowski told me where to find the dog food and I fed Boo-Boo and Za-Za and filled up their water bowl. The dogs wagged their plumed tails at me with excitement.

Mum filled the sink with hot, soapy water and washed up the dishes as she asked Mr Jankowski about how long he'd lived on Kira Island (57 years) and about his family (two sons who lived on the mainland with their own children and came to visit at Christmas).

'Could you please dry up for me, Pippa?' asked Mum, as she wiped down the benches. For a moment, I felt annoyed with Mum. I didn't really feel like doing more chores for this man I hardly knew. I just wanted to go home and get my homework done so I could relax. I still hadn't finished painting my fairy-wren for our art project.

'No, Pippa, please don't worry,' said Mr Jankowski. 'I can do it later.'

Mum opened her mouth to protest, and I realised that she had been working hard all day. She probably just wanted to go home and rest too.

'That's okay,' I said, taking a tea towel. 'I don't mind.'

'Pippa is very happy to help,' said Mum, giving me a wink. 'And you need to stay off that ankle, Mr Jankowski.'

He finished the quiche and put his knife and fork down. 'Thank you so much, Jenna. That was the most delicious dinner I've had in ages.'

'A pleasure,' Mum said, taking the plate and washing it up. 'I'm so glad you enjoyed it.'

Mr Jankowski picked up the newspaper and examined my doodles. I suddenly felt embarrassed. I probably shouldn't have drawn on his newspaper, but it was all crumpled and old, as though it had been there for days.

'These birds are very good, Pippa,' said Mr Jankowski. 'Do you do a lot of drawing?'

'Yes, I'm almost always doodling on something,' I replied. I looked at Mum, remembering the day I was sent to the principal in terrible trouble for doodling a picture of my teacher, Mrs Marshall. Joey had added devil's horns and a tail to the drawing. Mum rolled her eyes.

'Pippa's *trying* to give up doodling during class time,' teased Mum. 'Probably without much success.'

'Don't give up doodling,' said Mr Jankowski. 'You have a real talent and the more you draw the better.'

I felt a rush of pleasure at his compliment.

'In art class at school we're all making different birds to stick on a big tree we've painted,' I explained. 'I'm painting a fairy-wren.'

Mr Jankowski looked wistful. 'I used to paint. But I haven't touched a paintbrush in months . . . not since . . . not since my wife died.'

91

'Perhaps it's time to dust off your brushes,' said Mum. 'It's something lovely you could do while your ankle is mending.'

Mr Jankowski gazed out the window, looking sad. Mum tidied away the newspapers and picked up the dead pot plant.

'I think this one can go in the bin,' she suggested. 'And is there anything else we can do for you while we're here?'

'No. No,' said Mr Jankowski. 'You've done far too much already. I don't know how I'll ever thank you both.'

'It's a pleasure.' Mum smiled at him. 'I'll pop back tomorrow to make sure you're all right.'

CHAPTER 6

FIRST CUSTOMERS

On Wednesday at school I couldn't stop thinking about my dog-walking business. I just hoped the posters were enough to get me a few clients. Perhaps I should pay for an ad in the local newspaper.

I hardly listened as more of my classmates did their speeches. Cici's was called 'Dress like you're already famous'. Ariana talked about the importance of pets and her cat, Bianca, which she'd had since she was a baby. I was so glad

Mrs Marshall didn't ask me to do mine. I was far too distracted.

At lunchtime, all the year five students gathered under the big old fig tree to eat our lunches. We sat cross-legged in the shade.

Olivia, Sienna, Tash and Willow were excited about a movie they were going to see on Saturday.

'You guys should come with us,' suggested Olivia. 'You'll love it. It's about a girl who magically travels back in time to an olden day circus.'

'It has lots of cute animals too,' added Willow.

'It sounds great, but I promised to help Mum on the weekend,' I said.

Alex, Rory, Marcus, Sam and Joey were playing with gloopy balls of brightly coloured slime. They squeezed it between their fingers, tossed it in the air and threw it at each other.

'Catch, Pippa,' said Alex, lobbing a lump of

luminous green slime at my head. I caught the slime ball and threw it back to him.

'Careful, Alex,' I replied, with a grin. 'That nearly ended up in my pasta salad.'

The Sassy Sisters wriggled slightly apart from the others, away from the flying slime.

'Your talk was great today, Cici,' said Meg. 'I'm glad I haven't been chosen yet. I hate giving speeches in front of the whole class.'

'Me too,' I said. 'Mine's so bad I think I have to throw it out and start again.'

'Speaking of "Dress like you're already famous" . . .' said Cici, producing a parcel from her bag. It was wrapped in brown paper and tied up with red satin ribbon with a sprig of rosemary tucked into it. Cici was one of those people who always takes extra care wrapping presents so that even something as simple as brown paper looked special.

'What's that?' I asked Cici. 'Is it someone's birthday?'

Cici grinned at me with delight. 'It's not a birthday, but it is a little surprise. It's for you. Open it.'

Cici handed me the parcel. I sniffed the rosemary appreciatively. I couldn't believe that Cici had brought me a present for no particular reason. I thought back to what I'd said about her to Zoe on Monday. She was so lucky, but she was also warm-hearted and generous.

'Thank you, Cici,' I said, as I began to unknot the ribbon.

Inside the wrapping was a white T-shirt with handwritten calligraphy in turquoise fabric paint on the back. The writing said:

Pippa's Perfect Pooch Pampering
Dog walking and grooming

'Wow!' I said.

'I made it for you with the fabric pens Mum bought me,' said Cici. 'I thought you should have a uniform for your own business. So you look really professional.'

'That's a brilliant idea,' said Charlie.

'I love the little doggy paw print,' said Meg.

Cici laughed. 'Well, actually, I spilled a blob of paint, so I turned it into a paw print.'

I felt a wave of gratitude rush through me. How thoughtful of Cici to go to so much trouble for me and my little business. I gave her a hug.

'It's beautiful, Cici,' I said. 'I'll wear it this afternoon when I walk Hercules. Maybe lots of people will see me wearing it and I'll get even more customers!'

After school I raced to the cafe, only pausing to gaze longingly into the window of the surf shop. The three swimming costumes were still there. I imagined walking in with a pile of ten-dollar notes and buying the cobalt-blue-and-white costume.

No time to daydream. I had to get walking my first customer.

At the cafe I changed into my new dog-walking uniform. I wore my handpainted T-shirt with denim shorts, runners and a navy cap. It made me feel very professional.

I went upstairs to find Jason. Our apartment was a disaster zone. I couldn't imagine how the place could possibly be ready to move into on the weekend.

Daniel and Miguel were in the room that was to be our bathroom, banging and drilling.

'Come and see our new bathroom, Pipkin,' said Mum. Her cheeks were flushed with excitement. 'It's nearly finished. It even has a door!'

The timber door was no longer chipped or pale-pink. It was painted glossy white and looked as though it was brand-new. Behind it was an airy, whitewashed room with navy-blue floor tiles and double windows looking out over the turquoise water of the cove.

Under the windows was a deep, free-standing bath with a timber vanity to the left, painted the palest duck-egg-blue. To the right was the shower and the toilet. Miguel was drilling a hook into the wall where the handtowel would hang while Daniel swept up the sawdust from the floor. They both gave me a grin.

'It looks great,' I said to Mum. 'Does that mean we're really nearly finished?'

'You bet, Pipkin,' said Mum, kissing the top of my head. 'It's going to be a big weekend. All our new furniture is being delivered on Saturday morning super-early.'

'That is so exciting,' I said, feeling much cheerier. 'I can't wait to have our own proper home again. And see the apartment filled with furniture.'

Daniel and Miguel exchanged a dubious look.

'We'd better get cracking then,' said Daniel. 'There's still a lot to do before Saturday morning.'

I looked around at the mess in the other rooms. Every room had sawdust and shavings on the floor. Bella's room was half-painted a pale green and there was no door hanging in her doorway. Harry's room had a door with patchy orange paint and bare, sanded wood.

My soon-to-be bedroom was stacked with empty cardboard boxes from various bathroom fittings and there was a pile of broken tiles and offcuts in the corner. Jason had sawhorses set up with an old peeling purple door laid down across them. He was sanding the paint off it with an electric sander. The noise and the dust were terrible.

It seemed impossible that everything would be ready for us to move in by the weekend. I hoped Mum wouldn't be devastated if it didn't get finished in time.

'Hello, Pippa,' said Jason, turning the sander

off. 'Hope you don't mind me using your bedroom as a workroom!'

'No, that's fine,' I said. 'Although I can't believe I'll finally be sleeping here in a few days.'

'Fingers crossed,' said Jason. 'We'll do our best. Thanks for offering to take Hercules for his walk. He's really looking forward to it.'

'Me too,' I said.

'He's hiding in the living room,' said Jason. 'I think he'll be glad to escape the noise for a while.'

Hercules was lying asleep on a rug in the corner of the living room next to the builders' tools and bags. I don't know how he managed to sleep through all the racket. He jumped up and did a little prance when I walked in, his tail wagging and his pink tongue lolling.

'Come on, boy.' I clipped his lead onto his collar and Hercules followed me down the stairs, his huge paws taking three or four steps at a time.

I had just started walking out the front door when I heard Mum calling after me. She had a piece of paper in her hand.

'Pipkin, not so fast,' said Mum. 'You had a couple of phone calls today while you were at school.'

My heart thumped with anticipation. 'Are they dog-walking bookings?'

'Looks like it,' said Mum, with a grin. 'And they want you to start right away.'

I read the notes that Mum handed me.

Mrs Riley rang. Can you please walk her old labrador called Biscuit starting today. Pick up address 13 Victoria Rd at 3.30 pm.

Anna Ricci called about walking Rufus the schnoodle puppy and pooper-scoopering her garden. Today 3.30 pm at 27 Tower St.

'Two new customers! Hurray!' I said. 'That's brilliant news.'

'Can you please ask one of the other girls to go with you?' said Mum. 'It will be too hard for you to walk all those dogs on your own at once. Besides, I'd feel better if you were with someone in case you get into trouble with a strange dog.'

I thought for a moment. 'Charlie said she could help me. And she's great with dogs. I'll give her a call.'

'And don't forget you still need to walk Summer,' said Mum. 'You forgot this morning. Perhaps you can take her after you walk the other dogs?'

'Sure,' I said, impatient to be off.

I quickly rang Charlie and arranged to meet her outside the house of Rufus the schnoodle.

I was about to leave with Hercules, but then I had a better idea. Why didn't I just take Summer now with the other dogs to save time? Especially as I had Charlie to help me. I sprinted back to the cafe, grabbed Summer and her lead and set off.

Summer, as usual, was so excited she leapt around, licking Hercules on the nose and getting herself all tangled up in her lead. Hercules was patient and trotted along beside me beautifully.

'*Heel*, Summer,' I said sternly. She soon calmed down and stopped bouncing around like popcorn in a hot pan.

The first stop was 27 Tower Street, which was the closest address to the cafe. It was on a street that ran steeply up the hill towards the escarpment where Charlie lived with her family.

On the edge of the ridge was a grand mansion with a stone tower. Mum says it was used by the owner to watch out for his merchant ships coming into the harbour over a hundred years ago, and that the street was named after it. The house I was looking for was the converted stone barn right next door.

Charlie was walking down the road from the hill above with her two dogs, Robber and Bandit, who woofed with excitement to see us. They are shaggy black-and-white border collies with black masks across their eyes so they look like cartoon burglars.

'Why don't I hold all the dogs while you go in and pick up the pup,' suggested Charlie.

So I handed Hercules and Summer over to Charlie, pushed open the gate and went in. I recognised the family as soon as they opened the door. It was Rufus the black, curly-haired puppy who'd run away, Carlo the toddler and his mum with the big watermelon tummy.

'Hello, I'm Pippa Hamilton,' I said. 'I'm here to pick up Rufus for a walk. Although we did meet on the beachfront the other day when Rufus escaped.'

'Yes, I remember, Pippa,' she said. 'I recognised you on the poster in the pet shop. I'm Anna Ricci, and you know Carlo and Rufus.'

Carlo was hiding behind his mum's legs, but he looked up at me with big black eyes. Rufus wasn't interested in me at all. He was desperate to get out to the street to play with Summer, Hercules, Bandit and Robber.

Anna handed me Rufus's red lead. Rufus took the lead in his mouth and tugged me forward as if to say 'I'm a big boy. I can walk myself!'.

'It would be great if you could clean up the poos in our garden after the walk,' said Anna. 'And don't forget that Rufus can be an escape artist, so please don't let him run away.'

'Don't worry,' I said. 'I'm used to our puppy, Summer, and she gets up to all sorts of wicked mischief.'

Charlie and I set off with our charges, although it was a little trickier than I'd expected. Robber and Bandit were used to walking together, but Summer and Rufus refused to walk calmly when they could roll and tumble and play instead. Hercules had very long legs, while Rufus and Summer had short puppy legs, so it took longer than I'd expected to walk to Biscuit's house because I had to keep stopping to untangle them all.

'Why don't I take Hercules?' suggested Charlie. 'And you take the puppies?'

This plan worked better.

Once again, Charlie held all the dogs while I went and knocked.

The front door was opened by an older woman with steel-grey, bobbed hair and a stern face. Sitting at her feet was a plump, golden labrador.

'Mrs Riley?' I asked. 'I'm Pippa and I'm here to collect Biscuit for a walk.'

'You're late,' said Mrs Riley severely. 'I've been waiting for you. I was just about to ring to see where you were.'

I felt a wave of hot embarrassment. This wasn't off to a good start.

'Sorry, Mrs Riley,' I apologised. 'I had to stop by and pick up my other customer, Rufus, and he's been a little boisterous.'

Mrs Riley looked over at Charlie with her collection of dogs on leads.

'Make sure you give Biscuit a long walk,' said Mrs Riley. 'The vet says she needs to lose weight and I'm not paying you to let her lie around.'

Biscuit promptly lay down at her mistress's feet, looking completely exhausted before we'd even started.

'Yes, of course,' I said, trying to sound and look professional in my uniform. 'I'll make sure she has a good walk.'

'Hmm,' replied Mrs Riley. 'And don't let those boisterous little dogs bother her. Biscuit is ten years old, which is an old lady in dog years. I'll expect you back in one hour precisely.'

I felt a little scared by how stern Mrs Riley had been. I hoped the puppies wouldn't make us late because I didn't want another lecture.

Charlie and I set off, walking along the ocean esplanade to Pelican Park with three dogs each. Well, at least Charlie and her dogs walked. I had to drag Rufus, Summer and Biscuit along behind me.

'Heel, Summer,' I implored as I coaxed the three of them along. 'Hurry up, Biscuit.'

But my team soon became used to walking together and I began to enjoy strolling along in the afternoon sunshine, chatting to Charlie. The turquoise waves rolled in, breaking on the powdery white sand. A cool breeze stirred the palm fronds, smelling of salt and coconut oil. This was easy. What could possibly go wrong?

CHAPTER 7

PELICAN PARK

Pelican Park is at the northern end of Kira Beach, up past Mimi and Papa's house. The park is my favourite place to walk Summer because it has a shallow, clear lagoon fringed with reeds and a sandy beach where Summer loves to splash and play. Ancient hoop pines and palm trees provide shade and, best of all, it is completely fenced so the dogs can run off their leads.

Charlie unclipped her dogs at once. Bandit,

Robber and Hercules ran and chased each other, splashing through the shallow water. A flock of pelicans soared into the air and settled on the ruins of an old jetty. Other dogs were swimming and chasing balls along the beach.

I let Biscuit off her lead and she immediately flopped down in a small hollow in the sand, panting for breath. I unclipped Rufus and Summer and they began tumbling and rolling on the beach, clouds of sand billowing up around them. Soon Rufus had sand smudged all over his black face like icing sugar.

Summer splashed into the crystal lagoon. Rufus was more cautious, sniffing the edges and dipping first one paw, then all four paws in the shallow water.

'Don't they look like they're having fun?' said Charlie.

'Yes,' I agreed. 'Especially poor Biscuit. I suppose I better make her walk some more.'

'Good luck with that,' replied Charlie, with a chuckle. 'Biscuit looks like she doesn't intend on moving anywhere.'

Charlie was right. I coaxed and cajoled, but Biscuit just closed her eyes and pretended to sleep. I grabbed Biscuit by the collar and tried to drag her to her feet. She rolled over onto her side with her legs stretched out straight. She was far too heavy for me to lift.

'Come on, Biscuit,' I cried in despair, hauling at her collar again. 'Get up.'

Robber and Bandit came racing over and sniffed at Biscuit. Robber crouched down watching Biscuit intently.

I was then distracted by Rufus and Summer, who had stopped splashing in the shallows and were stalking two energetic Jack Russells. The terriers were digging a huge hole, sand cascading behind them like a waterfall.

'Those Jack Russells are trying to dig their way to China,' Charlie said, giggling.

Summer and Rufus darted in to join in the digging frenzy. The two pups scrabbled their paws frantically, sand flying everywhere. The Jack Russells growled a warning, chasing the pups out of their hole with a loud bark.

Summer and Rufus rolled on their backs, whimpering and whining, their eight legs waggling in the air. Hercules decided the safest place was leaning against the back of my leg. Biscuit gave a loud snore from her nest. This walk wasn't going to plan at all.

'Rufus and Summer, come here,' I ordered. 'You're supposed to be running, not lolling around. Come on Biscuit, get up.'

Of course, none of the dogs paid any attention to me. They continued to quake, snore and whimper. Bandit crouched beside the puppies, assessing the situation.

Robber and Bandit had clearly decided that I was a useless dog wrangler. Border collies are super-intelligent, bred to herd sheep and cattle, and to figure out what their humans need them to do. Both dogs sprang into action. Robber pounced forward with a loud bark and a warning nip at Biscuit's rump.

Biscuit struggled to her feet and waddled off towards the other dogs. Working as a team, the two border collies rounded up first Biscuit, then Hercules, then Rufus and Summer. They kept them in a tight pack, then raced them around and around and around in large sweeping circles. If any of the dogs slowed down they were encouraged to keep moving with a loud bark and a firm nudge. Gradually they gathered in a few extra dogs, including the Jack Russells, until they had mustered a herd of eight dogs of various sizes and breeds, all galloping along together.

Charlie laughed as she proudly watched her clever pets. 'And that's how it's done,' she crowed. 'Dog walking by the experts. It should be Robber and Bandit that are earning the pocket money.'

'Absolutely,' I replied. 'There's no way I could have made Biscuit get up and moving like that. No wonder she's so chubby.'

'Too many biscuits for Biscuit,' joked Charlie.

When Robber and Bandit had decided that the other dogs had received sufficient exercise, they slowed the pace and after one last circuit, brought the group back to us.

Biscuit collapsed back into her sandy hole, wheezing with exertion. Summer and Rufus flopped down on the ground, each laying their head on one of my feet. The other dogs peeled off to their various owners. Bandit and Robber looked up at us, their tongues panting and their tails wagging madly as if to say 'Did you see that? How clever are we?'.

'Yes, you are brilliant,' said Charlie, rubbing them around their ears. 'What good, hard-working girls. I think you both deserve an absolutely humungous bone tonight.'

I gave Summer and Rufus a pat too, then Hercules charged up and headbutted my thigh, begging for a snuggle.

'Isn't it amazing how Robber and Bandit just know how to herd?' I said. 'It's not like you've trained them to round up sheep for you.'

Charlie chuckled as she scratched Robber behind the ear. 'When we were little, they used to round up all five of us kids and herd us into the kitchen when we were being too slow coming for dinner. Robber used to nip us on the bottoms as if we really *were* sheep.'

'*Ouch!*' I laughed. 'That must have looked so funny.'

Charlie rubbed her bottom ruefully. 'Yep. Mum said the dogs were the best help ever with five children to look after. But thankfully she soon taught them that their job *wasn't* to nip and steer us around the house.'

We made a fuss of all the dogs until our arms ached with patting. Then I threw a few sticks into the lagoon for Hercules to give him some extra exercise.

I checked my watch. 'Job done. So now it's time to take them home. I still have to pick up all the puppy poo in the Riccis' garden.'

'And a couple here,' Charlie reminded me, as she waved towards Hercules sniffing around for a good place to poo in the reeds.

'Great,' I moaned, as I unknotted one of my plastic bags. 'Hercules does the most enormous poos in the world.'

After I'd cleaned up their messes, we caught each dog and clipped their leads back on. Then we set off home, the dogs trotting beautifully beside us. Rufus finally became so tired that I had to carry him the rest of the way.

We dropped off Summer and Hercules at the cafe, then Biscuit to her home. Mrs Riley handed me a crisp ten-dollar note and asked me if I could walk Biscuit again tomorrow. Of course I said yes. The money felt wonderful in my fingers for about one minute, but then I realised I really should give it to Charlie.

'This is for you, Charlie,' I said, handing her the note.

Charlie pushed the money back into my hand. 'It's your money, Pippa. I was just keeping you company and walking my own dogs.'

'No, we both did the same amount of walking, so we should go halves in the money,' I said. 'You take this and I'll take the money for Rufus. Besides, I couldn't have exercised Biscuit without Robber and Bandit's help!'

Charlie took the money. 'If you're sure. But I feel bad because I know how much you need that new cossie.'

'We'll earn more money,' I said optimistically. 'Can you help me again tomorrow?'

'Absolutely,' said Charlie. 'It was fun.'

I waved Charlie off, then walked Rufus back to the Riccis' house. Rufus licked me on the hand as I patted him goodbye.

'He's saying thank you for the lovely walk,' joked Anna, as she took the lead from me.

Anna showed me where they kept a bucket and spade and I whizzed around the garden, picking up all the puppy poos and popping them into the compost bin. I washed my hands under the hose, then collected a pile of puppy and toddler toys and stacked them neatly on the back terrace. When everything was tidy, I knocked on the back door.

'You've done a wonderful job,' said Anna. 'Rufus is completely unconscious in his bed. He hasn't been this quiet for weeks.'

'Brilliant,' I said. 'And I've cleaned up the garden, so I'm all finished now.'

'Thanks so much, Pippa. Can you walk Rufus again tomorrow at the same time?'

'Yes, sure.' I waited expectantly for Anna to pay me.

'Well, we'll see you then,' she said. 'Bye, Pippa.'

I shuffled from foot to foot, not sure what

to do. Should I ask her to pay me? That seemed rude. I hadn't thought that I might have to ask for the money.

'Um,' I said, mustering the courage to remind her. But I couldn't say it. 'Bye.'

Anna turned around and closed the door. I stood there for a moment, outside on the back terrace. Should I knock on the door again and just blurt out 'You owe me fifteen dollars!'?

I couldn't believe that after all that walking and pooper-scoopering I hadn't earned a penny.

Suddenly the door flew open, and there was Anna looking embarrassed. 'I'm so sorry, Pippa. I completely forgot to pay you,' she said. 'My brain has turned to mush with this pregnancy.'

She handed me three five-dollar notes. I grinned with relief as I took the money.

'Thanks so much, Anna. I'll see you tomorrow.'

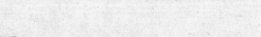

Back at the cafe, Mum had finished for the day. All we needed to do was drop off a basket of leftover food for Mr Jankowski on the way home. She had packed up half a tandoori-chicken pie, salad and pear-and-raspberry bread.

Boo-Boo and Za-Za greeted us with bois-terous yapping as we arrived at the front door. When the door opened they raced straight to me and sniffed all over my shoes and socks, checking what doggy scents they could smell.

'My apologies for the racket,' said Mr Jan-kowski, leaning on his crutch. 'They have severe cabin fever being locked up at home all day with only me for company.'

Mum looked at me. I sighed inwardly.

'Pippa could –' began Mum.

'Would you like me to take them for a quick walk around the block, Mr Jankowski?' I asked, biting the bullet.

'That would be wonderful, Pippa,' said

Mum gratefully. 'I'll just make up this meal for Mr Jankowski.'

So once again I was walking dogs. The Pomeranians had tiny little legs so they were very slow, especially as all they wanted to do was sniff everything and wee. It felt like a long walk around the block as I tugged on their leads and begged them to keep walking. When I arrived back, the front door was open so I went down the hall to the kitchen. Mum and Mr Jankowski were sitting at the table, drinking a cup of tea and chatting.

Za-Za and Boo-Boo ran straight to their bowls and looked up at me as if to say 'Hurry up. We're hungry.'

Mum laughed. 'It doesn't take them long to get used to a new routine.'

I fed them and changed the water in their bowl.

Mum stood up and cleared away the teacups.

'Pippa, I can't tell you how appreciative I am

that you took the dogs for a walk,' said Mr Jankowski. 'I've been worrying about them not getting any exercise, and the doctor said it will be another day or so before I can hobble down to the cafe.'

I thought about Mr Jankowski trapped here all day with just the dogs for company. Then I thought about Boo-Boo and Za-Za locked up all day with just Mr Jankowski for entertainment. That would be pretty boring too.

'Would you like me to come over tomorrow afternoon and take Boo-Boo and Za-Za for another walk?'

Mr Jankowski scratched Boo-Boo behind the ears. 'They would love that, thank you, Pippa.'

When we arrived back at the caravan I sprawled onto Mum's double bed, cuddling up to Smudge. Smudge purred with contentment as she kneaded me with her paws. I felt as exhausted as Biscuit after all that walking.

But then I felt the bulge of the money in my pocket. I held my very first earnings from my very own dog-walking business. It was a wonderful feeling. I had fifteen dollars. Could I possibly make another forty-five by Saturday?

CHAPTER 8

BOXES OF STUFF

On Thursday morning, we all arrived early at the cafe. It was box delivery day, which was unfortunate because it was pouring with rain. It doesn't rain often on Kira Island, but when it does it is torrential. Mum kept peering out at the sky, hoping to see a break in the weather.

At eight o'clock, the truck filled with our boxes pulled up out the front. Two delivery men dashed back and forth, carrying box after box through the front door of the cafe and up the stairs to our apartment. The men were quickly soaked and grumbled as they splashed back and forth.

Mum stood at the top of the stairs and directed them where to stack all the different boxes. 'That one goes in the kitchen,' ordered Mum. 'That box goes in the far bedroom.'

Each box was taped shut and labelled with its destination and contents – *Pippa's room – books. Harry's room – clothes. Kitchen – saucepans. Bathroom – towels.*

Bella kept racing around and getting under everyone's feet. She was super-excited. 'Try to keep out of the way, Bella-boo,' said Mum. 'I'd hate a box to get dropped on top of you.'

Mum was looking frazzled as the boxes kept coming. She'd been up late the night before painting Bella's room with Papa, long after we'd gone to bed.

By eight-thirty a pile of boxes had been

dumped in every room and the delivery team had gone. Mum used a Stanley knife to open one of the boxes labelled 'Bella's room – toys'.

'Bella, why don't you start unpacking this one?' suggested Mum. 'It will be full of surprising old treasures.'

Mum turned to us and pushed her damp hair off her forehead.

'Harry and Pipkin, why don't you start unpacking one or two of your boxes before you go to school?' she suggested. 'You can put the books on your shelf and hang your clothes in your wardrobe. I'll help Bella.'

'Sure, Mum,' said Harry. He headed off to his room to start unpacking.

I went into my new room. All the rubbish had been cleared out and the floor was swept. It was a big empty space, except for five boxes that we'd packed in our old house ten months ago. They were stacked in the middle of the room with the tape cut open. I felt a mixture of excitement and anticipation. What exactly was inside?

The first two boxes held my books and art supplies. I pulled a few books out and stacked them in piles on the floor, but I was soon distracted reading the titles and the blurbs on the back. There were some beloved old favourites here.

Then I found a dog-eared scrapbook that I'd filled with tickets, programs and photographs of my old life back in London. I sat there, poring over the pictures of my school friends, Miranda, Ava and Lily – mucking around, playing hockey and horseriding in Hyde Park. And, of course, there were so many reminders of my dad. Photos of him teaching me how to ride my first bike, playing cricket in our garden and taking us to the zoo. Snapshots of holidays and birthdays and family dinners. It brought all the old feelings of homesickness and sadness rolling back.

I snapped the scrapbook shut and started pulling clothes out of another box. Jumpers. Jeans. Shirts. Heavy winter overcoats. A scarf and gloves that Dad had bought for me our last London winter. Lots of dark colours – navy, black and grey. There was nothing there that was at all inspiring. Some of the clothes looked too small already. It was just depressing. I picked it all up and shoved it back in the box.

So when Mum came in to tell me to go to school, I'd achieved virtually nothing except to make myself feel miserable.

Mum looked around my room in dismay. 'How did you go, Pippa?' she asked uncertainly. 'Did you unpack anything?'

No,' I replied, looking glum. 'It was all too hard.'

Mum took a deep breath, the one where I knew she was silently counting.

'Well, perhaps you'll have better luck after school,' she said. 'I do need you to try, Pippa.

Harry's already unpacked all his stuff, and Bella's really too young to help. I can't do everything by myself.'

Mum looked like she was going to cry. I gave her a hug.

'I'll do it this afternoon, I promise,' I assured her.

I went off to school feeling terrible. During the maths quiz I was so distracted I made heaps of silly mistakes. Olivia shot me a look of triumph when she topped the class. Olivia and I have a friendly competition each week to see who can come first. Normally we're pretty even, but she'd well and truly trounced me today.

At recess, everyone had to stay inside because of the rain, which drummed on the corrugated iron roof of the hall. Olivia, Tash and Willow were on the stage teaching Ariana how to do backbend kickovers. Alex, Sam and Rory were playing football with a lunchbox, tossing it back and forth.

'Watch out, Alex,' I snapped, as he nearly crashed into me.

'Sorry, Pippa,' he said, looking remorseful. 'I didn't see you guys there.'

Rory threw the lunchbox to Alex and they kept charging down the hall.

We perched on the side of the stage, our legs dangling over the edge. I told the girls about my complete lack of progress with unpacking the London boxes. 'I achieved absolutely nothing,' I moaned. 'I thought unpacking the boxes would be exciting, like Christmas. But my old clothes were dark and daggy. It was no fun at all.'

'That's such a shame, Pippa,' said Meg.

'Hmm,' said Cici, with a thoughtful look. 'Sounds like you need a little bit of professional help.'

My day only got worse after recess, when Mrs Marshall announced it was time for another round of inspiring speeches about our passions. She turned and looked straight at me. I tried to duck my head.

'I think we'll start with Pippa today,' she said.

I felt my face turn pale and then red. With all the dog walking, helping at the cafe and the unpacking, I'd done nothing about my speech for days, except for the poor attempt I'd made in class last week.

I gabbled. 'Mrs Marshall . . . I . . . I . . .'

Meg sensed my panic and shot up her hand. 'Pippa's not feeling very well today, Mrs Marshall,' she said. 'But I'm happy to take her turn.'

This was a huge sacrifice because I knew Meg didn't want to speak in front of the class any more than I did.

Mrs Marshall looked at me with concern. 'Do you need to go to the nurse, Pippa?'

'Thanks, Mrs Marshall, but I'll be okay in a little while,' I said, trying to look both sick and brave at the same time.

'I'll let you off today, but you'll be the very first speaker tomorrow, is that understood?' asked Mrs Marshall, looking suspicious. 'You've had all week to prepare.'

'Yes, Mrs Marshall.' I made a mental note to rewrite my speech this afternoon after school. Actually, after walking the dogs and unpacking my boxes and helping Mum. Now I really did feel sick.

'Thanks so much, Meg,' I whispered as she stood up. 'You're a total lifesaver.'

Meg gave me a quick thumbs-up sign. Her hands were shaking as she gathered her palm cards. I smiled to give her confidence. Meg stood out the front and took a deep breath.

'My passion is saving the planet, especially our amazing wildlife,' began Meg, her voice a little wobbly. 'You might think this is too big a job for an eleven-year-old girl. But even something as simple as not using plastic bags, cling wrap or plastic bottles can make a huge difference.'

Meg looked around, her eyes alight with enthusiasm. She was so passionate that she forgot to be shy.

'Kira Island is so beautiful, with lots of really special marine life, such as dolphins, sea turtles, whales and sharks,' continued Meg. 'Did you know that every plastic bag you use could kill a turtle or a dolphin? Every year, over one million seabirds and one hundred thousand marine mammals die from plastic in the oceans. They get entangled in plastic and drown, or accidentally eat it. It makes me so sad to think that humans are responsible for destroying our natural environment and endangering animals.'

Mrs Marshall nodded in agreement.

'Did you know that more than two million plastic bags are used every minute?' asked Meg.

'Did you know that more than sixty million plastic bottles are thrown away *every day*? That's billions every year. The ocean is drowning in plastic waste and we can *all* do something to stop it.'

Meg paused for effect, looking around the room.

'Please, for the sake of our ocean and our planet, *refuse* plastic bottles, *reuse* cloth shopping bags, pick up rubbish if you see it and *recycle* plastic whenever you can. We can all make a difference and stand up for what we believe in. Thank you.'

Everyone in our class clapped enthusiastically.

'Well done, Meg,' said Mrs Marshall. 'That was an excellent speech and a timely reminder that small things can make a huge difference.'

Meg flushed bright red and sat down. Cici and Charlie clapped her on the back as she squeezed past them.

'That was fantastic, Meg,' I whispered. 'You were the best speaker yet.'

'I'm just glad it's over,' she whispered back. 'I hate getting up in front of everyone.'

'You didn't sound nervous at all,' said Charlie.

'And you totally saved Pippa,' said Cici, looking at me. 'Mrs Marshall will be expecting a *brilliant* speech from you tomorrow!'

CHAPTER 9

DOGGY DISASTER

I couldn't wait for school to be over so I could walk the dogs. When the bell rang, the four of us raced down the main piazza towards the cove. Thankfully the rain had finally stopped, leaving the air hot and steamy. The cobbles were glistening wet and there were small puddles everywhere.

'The sun's coming out,' said Meg.

'Do you want to go for a swim this afternoon?' asked Cici.

'Absolutely,' said Meg.

'I definitely can't,' I said. 'I have to walk all the dogs, then unpack my boxes, then help Mr Jankowski, *then* rewrite my speech for tomorrow. I'll be lucky to get any sleep.'

Cici laughed. 'That's a super-busy afternoon, Pippa.'

'I'll help you walk the dogs again,' said Charlie. 'I can meet you at the Riccis' house at half past three?'

'Sure,' I said. 'Thanks so much, Charlie. But can you make it three-forty? I need to walk Boo-Boo and Za-Za on the way, then I'll pick up Biscuit first so Mrs Riley doesn't get cranky again.'

'What time will you be at Pelican Park?' asked Cici. 'I'll come and meet you there with Muffin.'

'Great!' I said. 'We'll get there about four o'clock – that is, if we can get Biscuit there without stopping for a nap!'

'That sounds fun,' said Meg. 'Neptune the

sea cat won't want to go, but I'll come to keep you company.'

There was no time for dawdling today. I raced over to Mr Jankowski's house so I could take Boo-Boo and Za-Za for a speedy walk around the block. Both Mr Jankowski and the dogs were so pleased to see me.

As I walked the Pomeranians I racked my brains, trying to think what I could write my speech on for tomorrow. Nothing came to me. I had a quick chat with Mr Jankowski about art when I dropped the dogs back. I got the feeling that he would have loved to talk for longer, so I had to explain that I was in a hurry today.

Then it was back to the cafe to change into my uniform, collect Hercules and Summer, then the other dogs, then power walk along the esplanade to Pelican Park.

After the heavy rain, the lagoon was full of water the colour of milky tea. The sand flats were submerged and there were muddy puddles on the grass. A flock of pelicans paddled on the deeper water.

People were taking advantage of the clear weather to exercise their pets in the fenced park. There were dogs of all colours, breeds and sizes – sniffing and scratching, racing and chasing. An elegant woman in a floral dress and a broad, straw sunhat strolled past, pushing a navy pram. In the pram, instead of a baby, there were two chihuahuas, each wearing diamante collars and snuggled down on a flannelette blanket. The dogs yipped loudly from the safety of their stroller.

'Look at those chihuahuas,' said Cici. 'They look like fashion models. She should be carrying them in an expensive designer tote bag instead of pushing them in a pram.'

'You need to get Muffin a sparkly necklace,' suggested Meg, with a grin. 'Muffin's collar is spoiling your image as the best-dressed dog walker on Kira Island.'

'Why, thank you,' said Cici, flicking her black hair over her shoulder. 'However, I think Muffin looks much better with simple crimson leather.'

Cici, of course, couldn't go anywhere without looking gorgeous. She was wearing the pretty white sundress with the blue and orange embroidery that her mum had bought as a present. The rest of us were wearing shorts, T-shirts, caps and runners.

Biscuit flopped in the soft sand to have a nap. Rufus and Summer tumbled and rolled over and over in a wriggling mass of paws and tails. One white pup, one black pup. Bandit and Robber raced around trying to steal a ball from a German shepherd.

A huge shaggy Saint Bernard gambolled up to sniff at Hercules. Hercules was thrilled to discover a playmate nearly as big as he was. I unclipped his lead and the two darted off together, chasing a white butterfly. The Saint

Bernard reminded me of Dad, who'd sent us a postcard of one from Switzerland.

'My dad says Saint Bernard dogs are so brave,' I said. 'They dig through the snow to find people who are buried in avalanches. They've saved literally thousands of people in the Alps.'

'I don't think that Saint Bernard will be digging many people out of the snow on Kira Island,' said Cici. 'Maybe he can be trained to be a surf rescue dog instead.'

'Or maybe just a surfing dog,' said Charlie. 'There's a stand-up paddleboarder on the mainland who takes his three dogs surfing all the time. I've seen his photos. They're really cool.'

'I could train Summer to be a surfing dog,' I said. 'She loves the water and she's good at learning tricks.'

The girls and I stood and watched our charges having fun. Muffin wasn't sure whether to play with the big dogs, the puppies or the border collies.

Cici threw a ball across the grass and Muffin chased after it. *This is so easy,* I thought to myself. *And I've just earned another ten dollars towards my swimming costume!*

Rufus chased Summer. Summer chased Rufus. Then Summer spotted something amazing. She had discovered a deep, wide puddle filled with thick, oozy mud.

Summer took a flying leap and landed splat in the middle of the puddle. Mud sprayed everywhere. She began to dig.

'Summer, no!' I cried. Summer rolled over on her white, furry back, waving her four paws in the air.

Rufus cocked his head to one side, watching intently.

I ran as fast as I could to grab him. Rufus, of course, was much faster. He took a running start and flew straight into the mud puddle next to

143

Summer. The two puppies rolled and wrestled and wallowed, woofing with delight. Both of them were covered in thick black muck.

'*Summer*,' I shrieked. She looked up at me innocently with big brown eyes, as if to say 'What's all the fuss? We're just having fun!'.

'Oh, no,' I moaned. 'They're both *filthy*.'

'You'll have to give them a bath,' said Charlie. 'You can't take Rufus home looking like that, Anna would have a fit.'

'Summer, come,' I called firmly. 'Rufus, come.'

Both dogs looked at me, their heads cocked to one side, their ears pricked, deciding what to do.

'Summer, come here,' I ordered, in my sternest voice.

Summer came, racing towards us. Rufus chased her. When Summer reached us she veered around my legs and plopped down on her haunches behind me, her pink tongue lolling from her now black face. When Rufus reached us, he ran straight for Cici and jumped up. Two muddy paw marks streaked down her snowy-white dress.

'Rufus, no!' Cici screamed in horror. '*Look* what he's done to my new dress.'

Rufus jumped again, leaving another trail of sludge down Cici's beautiful dress.

'Rufus, down!' I ordered, lunging for his collar. 'Bad boy. Get down at once!'

Rufus slipped sideways out of my reach. Meg tried to wipe the mud away with her hands, but that only made the smear worse.

'Stop it, Meg,' begged Cici, nearly in tears. 'Pippa, this is your fault. You have to control those dogs.'

'I'm so sorry, Cici,' I said, feeling awful.

Charlie tried to grab Rufus but he wriggled out of her grasp. Judging that he was in deep trouble, Rufus decided to run for the hills. Charlie and I chased after him, calling his name. Rufus zigzagged back and forth, around hoop pines, between palm trees and through the undergrowth.

'Come on, Rufus,' I called winningly. I had him cornered in the long reeds beside the lagoon. 'Good boy.'

Rufus looked at me, then looked behind him. He chose freedom. Rufus splashed into the lagoon, which yesterday had been shallow. The pup was immediately washed off his feet, his little legs paddling back and forth frantically. The outgoing current caught him and he started drifting downstream towards the open sea.

'He's getting swept away,' cried Charlie.

How could I possibly explain to Anna and Carlo that I'd lost their precious pup?

I had to save Rufus. I yanked off my runners and socks and threw them on the sand. I splashed into the lagoon and waded out. Yesterday it had only been shin-deep and crystal clear. Now it was quickly over my knees, although I knew it would be shallow once I hit the sandbanks in the middle.

'Hurry,' called Meg.

'Be careful,' warned Cici.

I waded closer. I was nearly there. Rufus paddled faster.

I reached out, grabbed the pup under his tummy and scooped him out of the water. Rufus was shivering and whimpering as he cuddled into my chest.

'It's all right, boy,' I whispered into his furry ear. 'I've got you safe.' He licked me gently on my hand to say thank you.

I turned around, holding Rufus tightly, and waded back across the channel to the beach.

'Well done, Pippa,' said Charlie, giving me a squeeze around my shoulder.

'Look at you,' said Meg. I was soaked through and covered in watery mud. Rufus's fur was still matted with muck, despite his swim.

'I don't know who needs a bath more,' said Charlie, as she clipped his lead onto his collar. 'Pippa or Rufus?'

Cici laughed, her good humour returned. 'That would be *me* – or Summer.' She struck a pose, both arms held out wide to show how muddy she was. 'I think *definitely* me.'

'No,' I disagreed, with a chuckle. 'We can still see patches of white on you. Summer is completely black.'

'We should change her name to Winter, for a dark and stormy pup,' decided Meg.

We gathered up the other dogs and put them on leads – muddy Summer, Muffin, Robber, Bandit, Hercules and Biscuit, who was still snoozing in her sandy hollow.

I was holding Hercules, Summer and Rufus when the woman in the broad sunhat wandered back, pushing her pram. She stopped nearby and lifted out the two chihuahuas. With their bulging eyes, diamante collars and oversized ears, they reminded me of tiny aliens. The chihuahuas, one tan-and-white, one tan-and-black, took one look at our pack of dogs and began to yip and growl. The tan-and-white one darted towards Hercules, his tiny teeth bared in a snarl.

'Be nice, Wookie,' said the owner, in a sweet voice.

Wookie growled ferociously.

Hercules quaked with fright. He tried to hide behind my legs, but, of course, he was way too big. The tan-and-black chihuahua darted in on the other side, just like Bandit and Robber did when they were herding. Hercules yowled in dismay.

'Don't be a bully, Sookie,' said the woman lovingly, making no attempt to take either of them away. Sookie growled again and nipped at Hercules' toes. Hercules yelped and took off.

Not again, I thought. I held fast to Hercules' lead, before he could drag me flying behind him.

'Come on,' I yelled to the girls over my shoulder. 'Let's go.'

We ran to the gate of Pelican Park with our charges racing along beside us. We collapsed on the other side, with the park gate safely closed behind us.

'That was close,' Cici announced, with a grin. 'Hercules, the Great Dane, was nearly gobbled up by those pesky little chihuahuas.'

We all giggled. Hercules was still trembling with fright. I stroked his velvety nose. He leaned against my leg for comfort.

'Big, brave Hercules has met his match,' joked Charlie.

'The dreaded Wookie and Sookie,' added Meg.

'The only thing more terrifying than a pair of chihuahuas is a pair of fluffy Pomeranians – Boo-Boo and Za-Za,' I added. 'Hercules is way more scared of them.'

At last Hercules stopped quaking as I stroked his silvery-grey fur.

'Come on, boy,' I said. 'You've got to learn our Sassy Sisters motto – "Be brave! Be bold! And be full of happy spirit!" You can't let a couple of teensy chihuahuas bring you down.'

We laughed and joked some more as we walked down the esplanade beside the ocean.

One by one the girls peeled off. Cici went home to get changed out of her muddy dress, taking Muffin with her. Meg offered to deliver Biscuit back to Mrs Riley for me. I definitely didn't want another lecture from Mrs Riley for being late. Meg said she'd collect the money and give it to Charlie later.

Charlie volunteered to help me wash Rufus and Summer back at Mimi and Papa's house. We tied Hercules, Bandit and Robber out the front, then I grabbed a pile of old towels plus shampoo from the bathroom. Charlie tied up the two pups under the clothesline so they couldn't escape again. We fetched buckets of warm water and the hose, then rinsed and shampooed and rinsed again until both puppies were free of mud and beautifully clean and sweet-smelling.

We towelled them dry until their coats were fluffy and soft. Then we brushed them both to get rid of any knots.

'That's better,' said Charlie, snuggling Rufus. 'A perfect pooch-pampering makeover.'

'They both look adorable,' I said. 'You'd never believe they could cause so much trouble. This dog-walking business is more stressful than I'd thought.'

'No,' said Charlie, with a grin. 'It's been fun.'

I grinned back. 'Absolutely.'

Charlie took her dogs home while I delivered Rufus back to the Ricci family. Anna and Carlo opened the front door when I knocked. Carlo was peeking around his mum's legs, his thumb in his mouth.

'Sorry I took so long, Anna,' I apologised. 'I had to give Rufus a bath.'

I was going to explain about the puddle of mud when Anna interrupted me.

'That's perfect,' she said. 'Did you read my mind? I was going to ask you to give him a bath before the baby comes. It's too hard for me to do it right now.'

'Oh, right,' I said. 'Yes . . . I thought it might be nice to make him lovely and clean for the new baby.'

'You're so thoughtful, Pippa,' said Anna. 'And you've done a wonderful job of looking after Rufus for me.'

I felt thrilled at Anna's praise, although she might not have been so complimentary if she knew that I'd let Rufus get totally muddy and then nearly lost him when he ran away.

'Now I don't want to forget to pay you again,' said Anna. 'How much is it? Ten dollars for the walk and ten dollars for the bath?' Anna took some money out of her wallet. 'Here's twenty.'

I took the money for a moment, but then

I felt guilty. I handed one ten-dollar note back to Anna.

'I didn't really give Rufus a bath because I was being thoughtful,' I confessed. 'He and Summer rolled in a puddle of mud at the park, so he was totally filthy and I had to wash him.'

Anna grinned at me, her dark eyes twinkling. 'That's okay, Pippa. I thought Rufus might have been up to some mischief or other. But I really did want you to bath him today, so you can keep the money. It's so worth it for me to have a sweet-smelling, clean and exhausted puppy again.'

I clutched the money in my hand and bounced all the way home with Hercules and Summer. I had thirty-five dollars saved. Over halfway there with two more days to go!

But my elation didn't last long. I suddenly remembered my next job of the day was to unpack all those boxes before dinner. Maybe I could just throw it all in the charity bin?

CHAPTER 10

PROFESSIONAL HELP

I sat on the floor of my new bedroom, surrounded by half-unpacked boxes, piles of books and mounds of dark winter clothes.

I was rummaging through a box of decorations from my old bedroom in London – cushions in crushed pink velvet, beloved old toys missing eyes and ears, a jewellery box filled with trinkets and little knick-knacks from birthday parties. There were several framed photos of Miranda, Ava and Lily, which reminded me that I hadn't emailed them for weeks.

Where should I start? What should I do with all this stuff? I was wondering if I should creep up the secret ladder, hidden in the back of my wardrobe, to hide in my tower room and avoid the chaos. Then I heard a knock on my door and three familiar faces popped their heads in.

'How are you going with this huge mess?' asked Charlie, her green eyes twinkling.

'It's horrible,' I admitted. 'What are you three doing here?'

'Would you like some help?' asked Meg.

'Yes, please!' I said fervently. 'I would LOVE some help!'

'First things first,' said Cici, putting her backpack down on the floor. 'A dire emergency like this requires professional help, so I brought . . .'

With a flourish, Cici placed a box in my hands.

'Chocolate on chocolate cupcakes! I made

them when I got home from Pelican Park. Today, I think you need all the help you can get.'

'Cici, you're the best,' I said, taking the lid off the box and admiring the perfect creations inside.

'I know,' she said, popping her hand under her chin with a cute pout. 'Chocolate cupcakes can fix any drama.'

'Does this mean you've forgiven me for Rufus streaking you with mud?' I asked hesitantly. 'Is your new dress ruined?'

'No,' Cici assured me, with a grin. 'Luckily Mum knows a few tricks. She's concocted a magic potion, and the dress is soaking in it. She says it will be as good as new by tomorrow.'

The four of us sat on the floor, perched on my crushed velvet cushions, eating fluffy chocolate cupcakes topped with swirls of thick chocolate buttercream icing.

'These are seriously good,' said Charlie. 'A wicked combo.'

'Mmm,' I said, licking chocolate icing off my fingertip. 'I feel better already.'

'Brilliant,' said Cici, with a smile. 'Because we have a lot to do and Mum's picking me up in an hour. She wasn't going to let me come, but I told her it was an emergency.'

Cici looked around, assessing the chaos I'd created. It made Bella's dino-tail mess in the caravan look like nothing.

'What we need,' said Cici, 'is a plan.'

She took a quick peek in each of the various boxes. She's a neat freak and her room is always perfectly organised.

'Let's do the books first,' she suggested. 'That's the easiest place to start.'

Meg and I unpacked the two boxes of books into piles on the floor, then Charlie and Cici arranged them neatly on my shelves.

'I love these books,' said Meg, as we unpacked my well-thumbed copies of the Narnia series. Charlie scooped them up and carried them to the bookshelf before we could start browsing through the pages.

'Shall we arrange them by colour, topic or alphabetically by author?' asked Cici.

'I like mine by type of book,' I said. 'Old favourites, mysteries, pony books, classics, historical . . .'

Cici tweaked the books so that they looked good on the shelves, arranging them by size, stacking some horizontally and some vertically. The shelves filled quickly, looking warm and colourful.

'Don't books make a room look cheery?' I said.

When the books were all stacked we started on the box of decorations. Meg set up the photo frames on the shelves, together with my jewellery box. Charlie artistically arranged my old teddy bears, lop-eared bunnies and assorted fluffy toys on the very top shelf. Cici set the velvet cushions on the window seat.

'I think they need a little makeover,' she said, fluffing a particularly squashed one. 'They're not quite right for what you wanted your new room to be.'

At last we had just the two boxes of clothes to sort.

'I can't believe I brought all this stuff halfway round the world,' I complained, rifling through a pile of T-shirts. 'Some of these are way too small.'

'You've probably grown in the last few months,' said Charlie. 'All this fresh air and Kira sunshine.'

'They might fit Bella,' Meg suggested. 'Although she's more of a dinosaur suit kind of girl.'

'Let's sort everything into three piles,' suggested Cici. 'This pile is the clothes that are too small, which you can give to Bella or the op shop. This pile is things you'll definitely wear again. And this pile is stuff you're not sure about.'

The girls had fun holding up clothes against themselves and helping me decide what to keep. The op-shop pile steadily grew. The clothes-to-keep were neatly folded, and Cici and Meg stacked them in my wardrobe.

I held up an old, worn pair of jeans with a few holes in them.

'I loved these jeans,' I said sadly. 'I wore them nearly to death.'

'Chuck,' said Meg, gesturing to the op-shop pile. I tossed them on the heap, but Cici rescued them and held them up.

'You could cut these down into really comfy shorts,' she said. 'If we added some crocheted lace to the hem, they'd be super-cute.'

'I suppose it's worth a try,' I said, but it seemed like a wasted effort.

'I'll get some scissors from downstairs,' offered Charlie.

'No need,' said Cici, dragging over her backpack. 'I brought some along, as well as my fabric pens, some scraps of ribbon and lace and my sewing kit.'

I tried on the jeans and Cici drew a line where she thought she should cut them.

'Isn't that a bit short?' I protested.

'Not with the crochet border,' she assured me. 'I can do that in a few minutes.'

Cici opened her magic bag of tricks and pulled out a long strip of cream crocheted lace. She quickly stitched it around the hem of my old jeans. I tried them on again and twirled around. An instant pair of fun, new shorts.

'These are adorable,' I said to Cici.

She pulled another pair of old jeans from the pile.

'Wait till you see what we're going to do to these,' said Cici, snipping the scissors in the air. 'Flower power!'

She cut off the legs and we used Cici's fabric pens to decorate the shorts with flowers and leaves in pretty colours. When we were finished

I hung them on the window seat to dry. Then Charlie used the paints to write 'Joy' in rainbow colours on one of my old white T-shirts. Meg decorated another one with 'Fight for what you believe in'.

'This is so much fun,' I said, painting a hot-pink love heart on an old pale-blue T-shirt. 'When you arrived I was thinking I'd never get those boxes unpacked. Now we're nearly done and it's taken hardly any time at all.'

'Four pairs of hands make light work,' said Meg.

'And together, the Sassy Sisters can make any boring job fun,' added Charlie, with a smile.

Charlie and Cici finished folding my clothes away in the drawers in my cupboard. Meg took the empty cardboard boxes downstairs to the recycling bin while I packed all the reject clothes into a big bag to go to the op shop.

By the time Nathalie arrived to drive the girls home, we were finished. My room was tidy and all the boxes were gone.

'That's much better,' said Meg, looking around.

'I told you some professional help was all it took,' said Cici.

'Thanks so much, guys,' I said, hugging each of them goodbye. 'I just don't know what I'd do without you.'

CHAPTER 11

FRIENDSHIP

When we finally returned home to the caravan, I was exhausted. All I wanted to do was curl up in my bunk with Smudge and go straight to sleep. Mum made a simple cheese and chive omelette for dinner. I think she was pretty tired too, but neither of us was ready for bed yet.

The adventures of that afternoon had made me realise what my new speech should be about.

After dinner, I sat at the tiny dining table and

wrote it out. I read it aloud to Mum and practised on Summer. She sat with her head cocked
to one side, hanging on every word.

On Friday morning at school, when Mrs
Marshall called my name I was ready.

I stood out the front, clutching my palm
cards in sweaty hands. Everyone looked
at me expectantly. Mrs Marshall nodded to
let me know I should start. I took a deep
breath. I remembered Dad's public speaking
advice from when I had terrible stage fright at
our school talent quest audition and stood tall
with my shoulders back.

'There is something wonderful that inspires
me every day,' I began. 'It is something we all
enjoy. Yet we all take it for granted.'

I looked around at my classmates. The
faces that I'd known for only a few months,
but who had all touched my life in so many
ways. I smiled at Olivia, Sienna, Willow and
Ariana. I smiled at Alex, Joey, Sam and Rory.

'The wonderful thing in my life is friendship,' I continued. 'I am so lucky to have a group of friends who make me laugh, look out for me and make every day full of fun. We go kayaking and swimming, hang out together, sing songs, dance and tell jokes.

'Even more importantly, my very best friends are there for me all the time. Not just on the happy, fun days. But also on the days when I'm cranky, or sad, or life just isn't going my way. When times are tough, my friends are always there for me, to give a helping hand, to cheer me on and to bake me chocolate cupcakes.'

I grinned at Cici, Meg and Charlie. Cici gave me a thumbs up.

'Thank goodness for best friends. They're the best!'

Mrs Marshall beamed at me. 'Thanks for that terrific speech, Pippa. I'm glad you've made such fabulous friends on Kira Island. And I do hope that today is a happy, fun day, not a cranky day.'

I beamed back. 'Absolutely.'

After the other speeches had been given, we had an art session with Miss Annand to complete our class project. We all made the finishing touches to our individual birds, then carefully glued them onto the painted canvas. Some perched on branches or nestled among the leaves. Others flew high in the sky or huddled around the trunk. My superb fairy-wren was hovering on the topmost twig, surveying his kingdom below.

'Great work, Pippa,' said Miss Annand, as I glued him to his roost. 'I love your delicate fairy-wren, the colours are simply divine.'

Our bird project was left to dry in the art room. On Monday it would be hung in the school hall to brighten the walls. We washed up and then went to change into our swimming costumes.

Fridays are my favourite school day because we spend the afternoon kayaking. We do races and explore Kira Cove. We capsize just for fun or float around chatting. We splash each other and watch the dolphins swimming. There's nothing more peaceful than paddling across the turquoise water in the sunshine. Then, afterwards, it's the weekend and we usually have our Sassy Sisters meeting up in the tower room above my bedroom at the Beach Shack Cafe.

Today, though, Mum had banned us from going upstairs because the builders were working late. Plus, I would need to fit in my dog walking before the weekend could really begin.

After kayaking, we dragged our boats up onto the beach, then hosed them off behind the boathouse. Most of us stood around chatting for a while. Alex, Rory, Sam and Joey were playing tip on the sand. Sienna, Willow and Olivia were walking on their hands along the grass. Tash was helping Ariana to perfect her backbend kickovers.

Of course, I was still wearing my saggy old swimming costume. I tried really hard not to think about it. The Riccis had cancelled my walk with Rufus today because something had come up, so I'd just be walking Biscuit (along with Summer and Hercules). This meant I'd only earn another ten dollars, taking my total savings to forty-five dollars. So there was no way I'd have enough money by tomorrow to buy my new cossie before the sale ended. Somehow that didn't bother me as much as I thought it would.

I left the other girls so I could race off to pick up Biscuit, Hercules and Summer. Near the cafe, I saw Mr Jankowski sitting on a wooden bench overlooking the cove. The two Pomeranians were tied up at his feet. He had a sketchbook on his lap and was drawing the old boatshed, which was now the Beach Shack Cafe. It was the first time I'd seen him out of the house since his accident on Monday. I went over to say hello.

'You're drawing again, Mr Jankowski,' I said.

He smiled back at me. 'You and your mum inspired me, Pippa. I dug out my sketchbook to draw some scenes of Kira Island life. I haven't done any painting yet, but I can't wait to try it – the colours of the cove are exquisite today.'

I looked at his sketch of the boatshed. 'It's so good,' I said. 'I wish I could draw like that.'

'I've had a few more years' practice than you,' replied Mr Jankowski. 'But I'm a little rusty. It feels marvellous to hold a pencil again.'

Boo-Boo and Za-Za were jumping around at my feet, clamouring for attention. I bent down and patted them both. Today they weren't wearing their human clothes, just their ordinary leads.

'The dogs must be happy that you are up and about again,' I said.

'Poor Boo-Boo and Za-Za put up with me as well as they can,' said Mr Jankowski. 'They really belonged to my wife. I couldn't believe it when she bought these ridiculous dogs with their ridiculous names and dressed them up . . .'

'They're lovely dogs,' I said hurriedly.

Mr Jankowski stroked Za-Za's back. 'When my wife died she left a hole so big, it seemed impossible to fill it,' he said, his voice cracking. 'At first, Boo-Boo and Za-Za were the only reason to get out of bed.'

I nodded, not sure what to say.

'A few months ago, when you first opened, I wandered into the cafe and your mum gave me such a cheery welcome that I went back the next day,' said Mr Jankowski. 'A few days later, Zoe recommended banana bread with my coffee, so I've had that ever since.

'For months, every morning I've thought that if I can just make it to the Beach Shack Cafe, then maybe I can make it through the day,' he continued. 'If it wasn't for your mum and Zoe, I don't know what I would have done.'

I looked up and realised that his eyes were

brimming with tears. Poor Mr Jankowski. I couldn't imagine what it might be like to feel so sad and alone. Thinking of Mr Jankoswki made me feel so lucky to have Mimi and Papa, Mum, Harry and Bella, Zoe and, of course, my wonderful Sassy Sisters.

'I do know what you mean, Mr Jankowski,' I said softly. 'When we first moved here, I was really sad too. I missed my dad. He didn't die, but he moved away to Switzerland, leaving a huge hole in our lives. Mum and Zoe helped me so much – and all my friends, and keeping busy.'

Mr Jankowski and I smiled at each other. 'You know, Mr Jankowski, we do serve some other delicious food at the cafe besides banana bread,' I joked. 'One day you have to try the lemon cupcakes. They're incredible.'

Mr Jankowski laughed. It was the first time I'd seen him laugh and it transformed his face, making him look years younger. 'I might just do that, Pippa. It might be time to try something new.'

We said goodbye and I headed into the cafe.

Inside, I noticed that my old friend Mrs Beecham was sitting at her favourite armchair in the bookshop nook, waiting for her tea. She came in every afternoon for a pot of freshly brewed Prince of Wales tea and a cupcake. Sometimes she met one of her friends, while other days, like today, she sat on her own. She liked sitting in the book nook so she could see people coming and going and have a chat.

'Hello, Mrs Beecham,' I said. 'How are you today?'

'Splendid, Pippa,' said Mrs Beecham. 'How's your dance practice coming along? You know I'm looking forward to coming to your dance concert at the end of the year.'

'Not bad,' I said, although to be honest

I hadn't practised in ages. 'I've been pretty busy lately walking dogs and helping Mum.'

'I saw your poster by the front door,' said Mrs Beecham. 'Why are you walking dogs?'

I told Mrs Beecham about my swimming costume dilemma and how I decided to try dog walking.

'I think that is perfectly wonderful,' she said. 'When I was a young girl in Russia, I used to clean the ballet studio to pay for my dance lessons.'

Chatting to Mrs Beecham suddenly gave me a brainwave. I thought of her sitting here in the cafe all alone. And I thought of Mr Jankowski sitting outside all alone. Wouldn't it be wonderful if they could meet and become friends? They were two of my favourite customers, so surely they'd grow to like each other too?

'Mrs Beecham, I have a new friend I'd like you to meet,' I said hurriedly. 'Is it okay if he comes and joins you for a cup of tea?'

Mrs Beecham looked surprised and I was worried for a moment she was going to say no.

'His name is Mr Jankowski and he's recovering from a sprained ankle,' I explained. 'I think you'll really like him.'

'Well . . .' Mrs Beecham hesitated.

'He's right out the front, so I'll go and fetch him now,' I said, before she had a chance to say no.

Fortunately, Mr Jankowski was still sitting on the park bench, packing up his sketchbook and pencils into a satchel.

'I'm just heading back,' he said, untying Boo-Boo and Za-Za.

'I thought you might like to come in for a cup of tea?' I asked, waving my hand invitingly towards the cafe.

Mr Jankowski shook his head, as he struggled to his feet. 'Thanks, Pippa, but I might hobble home.'

I was so disappointed. It was such a clever

idea. I decided I wasn't going to give up that easily. 'We have delicious strawberry cupcakes today,' I wheedled. 'They're super-scrumptious. And you did say that it was time you tried something new.'

Mr Jankowski chuckled. 'All right then, Pippa. How could I resist such a kind invitation?'

I walked Mr Jankowski back to the cafe, with Boo-Boo and Za-Za trotting along. Zoe had served Mrs Beecham her tea in her favourite teapot covered in roses. I steered Mr Jankowski towards her.

'Mrs Beecham, have you met Mr Jankowski?' I asked. 'He's one of our regulars every morning.'

'No, I haven't,' said Mrs Beecham, with a kind smile. 'How do you do, Mr Jankowski?'

'Pleased to meet you, Mrs Beecham,' said Mr Jankowski.

'Mr Jankowski sprained his ankle, so he can't walk very far,' I explained. 'He usually sits out on the jetty, but I thought perhaps you wouldn't mind if he shared your table?'

'No, please don't trouble Mrs Beecham,' he said hurriedly, looking embarrassed. 'I can easily walk that far.'

'No, you mustn't tire yourself,' she replied, gesturing to the armchair opposite. 'Please, do join me. How did you sprain your ankle?'

I went to fetch Mr Jankowski a pot of tea and a strawberry-cream cupcake on a side plate. As I returned carrying the tray, I heard Mrs Beecham say, 'Please, call me Natalya.'

'And my name is Jakub,' he replied.

I felt very pleased with myself as I bounced off to fetch Hercules and Summer for their walk. My brilliant plan was going perfectly. It looked like Mr Jankowski may just have made a new friend.

CHAPTER 12

MOVING DAY!

It finally arrived. Saturday morning. Moving Day!

I was so excited I had barely slept all night. When Mum's alarm went off early in the morning I crept out of my bunk, careful not to wake Harry and Bella. It was still dark outside.

Mum popped the kettle on the stove to make tea. I looked around the cosy caravan that our family had lived in for months. Harry was asleep in the bottom bunk, his dark hair all tousled. Bella was curled up like an echidna in Mum's bed, cuddling her dinosaur tail. Summer and Smudge were snuggled up together in their bed under the dining table.

For a moment I felt a wave of sadness wash over me. This would be the last morning that my family woke up together in this little home. Even though sharing such a small space with Bella and Harry had driven me mad at times, it had been lovely too.

I thought of all the fun games of cards we'd played squished around the little table or sprawled out on Mum's bed. How easy it was to fetch a drink from the fridge without leaving your chair. And how much closer we'd become as a family since we moved to Kira Island.

Mum kissed the top of my head. 'I can't believe I'm saying this, but in a funny way I'm going to miss this squashy little caravan, Pipkin,' she said.

'Me too, Mum. It's been an adventure, hasn't it?'

'We have a new adventure starting today,' said Mum. 'Moving into our new home.'

I snuggled next to Mum as we drank a cup of tea, enjoying this peaceful time together. Mum looked around. The caravan looked super-tidy and rather bare. Yesterday, she had packed up lots of our stuff and moved most of it to the apartment. The last load was packed in boxes in the back of the car.

'Okay,' said Mum, taking a deep breath and finishing her tea. 'It's time to wake the others and get cracking. We have a huge day today.'

We certainly did. When we arrived the apartment looked very different from the building mess I'd seen a couple of days ago. Mum and Papa had finished painting Harry's room late last night. The apartment still had a strong smell of paint and sawdust. Mum flung open the French doors in the living room to let the fresh sea air blow through.

Our builders – Jason, Daniel and Miguel – were already there doing last-minute jobs. Daniel and Miguel were hanging three glass pendant lights over the kitchen bench while Jason was fastening chrome doorknobs on our freshly painted, glossy white doors.

'We're nearly there, Pippa,' Jason said to me.

We all helped to carry up our boxes from the car and stack them out of the way. Today Zoe was running the cafe downstairs with the help of her friend Lisa.

Mum had organised for our new furniture to be delivered on two small trucks which came over to Kira Island from the mainland on the 8 am ferry. They arrived at the boatshed a few minutes later.

'Where would you like all this?' asked one of the removalists.

'Just up here, please,' said Mum, waving them in through the cafe and up the stairs.

'Okay, lads,' he said. 'Let's get these trucks unloaded.'

The team of four burly removalists worked to carry in our beds, mattresses, Mum's desk, an antique chest, a comfy lounge, armchairs and a sideboard. Mum had found some old wooden dining chairs and side tables at the op shop, which she'd painted palest blue. In no time at all, our empty apartment was filled with furniture in beachy shades of coral-white, duck-egg-blue and sea-green.

Once the furniture was placed where Mum wanted it, we had loads more boxes to unpack. The task would have seemed insurmountable, but luckily we had friends.

Cici and her parents, Nathalie and Eric, dropped by. 'We've come to see if we can help, Jenna,' said Nathalie. 'And we brought a little something for Pippa's room.'

Her arms were filled with metres of sheer, filmy white material.

'I asked Mum if she had any material we could use to make a floaty canopy above your bed, Pippa,' said Cici. 'Just like that photo on your mood board.'

'You remembered,' I said, fingering the silky fabric. 'I've always wanted one. They look so tropical and dreamy. Thanks so much, Nathalie.'

Nathalie and Papa hung the material from the ceiling, draped over some bamboo rods. Eric had made a huge spinach and ricotta cannelloni for our dinner which he stored in the fridge.

Next, Meg popped by with her mum, Mariana. They set to work helping Mimi and Eric unpack the boxes of saucepans, crockery and cutlery into the kitchen cupboards.

'Helloooo,' called a voice coming up the stairs. It was Charlie and her mum, Jodie.

'Jenna, these are for you from our garden,'

said Jodie, holding out an armful of blue and white hydrangeas. 'Do you have a vase?'

'Will this do?' said Mimi, holding out a white jug. 'I've just unpacked it.'

Jodie filled the jug with water and arranged the flowers. She popped it in the middle of the dining table, which Papa had built for us from recycled timber.

'They look absolutely perfect there,' said Mum, beaming with delight. 'Look, the colour almost matches my chairs.'

'Now, what can we do?' asked Jodie.

'Pippa and I were just about to make up all the beds,' said Mum.

'Why don't I do that with the girls while you do something else,' suggested Jodie. 'Where are all the sheets?'

Mum hoisted up a basket of freshly washed linen and passed it to Jodie. We started in Bella's room. She'd chosen a new doona patterned with green, blue and red dinosaur heads – no surprises there. Mum's linen was snowy-white to contrast with the soft duck-egg-blue of her bedhead, armchair and ottoman. Harry's room was given a nautical flair with navy-and-white stripes on his doona with the odd pop of red.

'Come and grab some lunch, darlings,' said Mimi, sticking her head around the door. 'You must be starving after all your hard work.'

'Absolutely,' I said, feeling my tummy start to rumble.

In the kitchen, Mimi and Papa had made up a large platter of different finger sandwiches – egg-and-lettuce, salmon-and-cucumber and ham-and-tomato. We all enjoyed taking a break, sitting wherever we could find a spot.

Afterwards, Charlie, Meg, Cici and I went to tackle my bedroom.

Together we made up my new bed with crisp sheets, plump pillows and the paisley doona cover Mum had bought. I smoothed the turquoise and sea-foam-green cover so it sat perfectly. It looked nice, but it wasn't quite as I'd imagined it when I'd chosen it from the photograph. Something was missing.

Just then Mum came in, carrying a large cardboard box which she put down on the floor beside me.

'This is for you, Pipkin.' Mum beamed at me. 'I thought the girls might like to help you with it.'

'What is it, Mum?' I asked, burning with curiosity.

'It's some little presents for your room, to make it special for you, and to say thank you for all your hard work over the last few months. I know it hasn't always been easy.'

Mum hugged me close.

'Thanks, Mum,' I replied, with a thrill of pleasure. 'You're the best mum in the world.'

I used some scissors to slit the tape on top of the box. The top flaps sprung open. We all peered inside.

One by one I pulled out the treasures. On top was a textured white throw rug for the end of my bed. Next was a collection of cushion covers in sea-foam green, turquoise and a pop of watermelon pink to transform my old velvet cushions on the window seat. A stack of white wicker baskets were perfect for storing my bits and pieces, while a collection of seashells and starfish created a truly beachy vibe.

Lastly, I pulled out a turquoise bedside lamp with a white shade, just like the one in the photo I'd stuck on my wall. Mum had sourced all these presents to help me create my dream bedroom, inspired by the photos I'd collected on my mood board all those months ago.

The four of us had fun arranging my new knick-knacks. We transformed my room from bare and basic to beautiful – just like the stylish bedrooms in the magazines I'd pored over.

Finally we took down the old mood board because I didn't need it anymore. To hang in its place we created a collage on a pin board with all my favourite polaroid photos of Mum and Dad, Bella and Harry, Mimi and Papa, Summer and Smudge. And, of course, loads of photos of the Sassy Sisters – dressed up for parties, kayaking, singing up a storm, hugging each other and pulling super-silly faces. Papa hung it above my desk.

When we'd finished, Papa carried away his toolbox. The four of us stood in the middle of the room and admired everything. Warm afternoon sunlight streamed through my window, which was flung open to let in the breeze. Smudge was curled up asleep, snuggled in the throw rug at the end of my bed.

Cici grabbed some cushions from the window seat and arranged them artfully on my bed.

'That's better,' she said, tweaking the throw rug so it draped prettily. 'Now your room is absolutely perfect.'

'I can't believe it looks so different after just one day,' said Meg.

'It's so peaceful,' said Charlie. 'I can't wait to have a sleepover party here. We'll have the best fun.'

'I know,' I agreed, dancing a little jig of excitement. Just then Jason popped his head around the door.

'Do you like your new room, Pippa?' he asked.

'I *love* it,' I replied, twirling around with my arms outstretched.

'Good,' he said, with a grin. 'We're finishing up now. The job is finally done.'

I felt a little wave of sadness at the thought of our builders no longer being part of our lives. Jason was always quick with a smile and a joke. All three of them were so friendly and warm, proudly showing us their progress day by day. And they'd do anything to help us, as long as there was a cupcake or two as a reward.

'Oh,' I said. 'I guess we won't see much of you anymore.'

'Don't worry, Pippa,' said Jason. 'I'm not giving up my daily fix of Beach Shack Cafe coffee and delectable food. We'll be popping by all the time.'

I grinned at him. 'That's a relief. I'd miss Hercules too much.'

'Speaking of my huge goofy dog,' said Jason, 'thanks so much for looking after him for me this week. It was such a help that you took him for a walk every day, and he loved playing with all the other dogs.'

'That's okay,' I said. 'It was a pleasure, and I was walking Summer and Rufus anyway.'

'I know,' said Jason, fumbling in his back pocket. 'But I got you a little present.'

Another present? What could it possibly be? Jason pulled out an envelope and handed it to me. I was feeling totally spoiled today.

I opened the envelope to find a fun

thank-you note. Tucked inside was a photo of Hercules grinning and a card. It read:

KIRA ISLAND SURF SHOP
$20 Gift Voucher for
Pippa Hamilton

'Zoe said you were saving up for something special from the surf shop, so I thought you might like a little help,' explained Jason.

My heart fluttered with excitement. I'd forgotten all about the surf shop's sale and the swimming costume.

'Thank you *so* much, Jason,' I said. 'With this voucher, I'll be able to get the new cossie I've been saving up for.'

I checked the time. It was 4.30 pm.

'Come on, let's go,' said Cici. 'The shop closes soon. Quick!'

The four of us raced into the hallway, where

Mariana was helping Mum to stack towels, sheets and tablecloths into the linen cupboard.

'Mum, Mum,' I called. 'Can we go to the surf shop, *pleeeeaaase*?'

'What's up, Pipkin?' she asked. 'You look like you've just won the lottery.'

'I have,' I said. 'I've got enough money to buy my new swimming costume. But today is the last day of the sale and the shop closes at five o'clock.'

Mum shooed us out the door. 'Then you'd better hurry, girls! You don't want to miss out.'

CHAPTER 13

A LOVELY SURPRISE

The four of us ran all the way to the surf shop on the main piazza of Kira Cove.

Cici grabbed my arm. 'Pippa, look.'

The window of the surf shop was empty. The mannequins wearing the swimming costumes were gone.

'Do you think . . . do you think they've sold out?' I asked. My heart plummeted to the bottom of my stomach.

Charlie pushed open the door. 'Only one way to find out.'

Inside, one of the shop assistants was carrying a box out the back. Another was packing up the T-shirts from the sale table. I walked up to her.

'Can I help you?' she asked.

I took a deep, nervous breath. 'Yes, please. I wanted to look at the swimming costumes that were in the window. The ones on sale?'

'We've had a big run on swimming costumes this week,' she replied.

'Do you still have the floral one in cobalt-blue and white?'

'The one with the cute little tassels at the back?' she asked.

I nodded.

'I think we sold that one this morning, but let me check what we have left in your size.'

My mouth was dry with dread. It would be

too cruel to have worked so hard and to miss out by a few hours.

The sales assistant bustled out the back. The four of us looked at each other. Charlie crossed her fingers for luck.

It seemed to take forever for her to come back, carrying a pile of folded swimming costumes.

'These are the only swimming costumes I have left in your size,' she said. 'I'm not sure if the cobalt floral is there?'

'At least there's something left,' I said to the girls, trying to be positive.

The first costume on top was a navy-blue one-piece. My heart sank. I'm never buying another boring navy-blue costume ever. The next one she showed me had a fluorescent orange and yellow hibiscus pattern – not my favourite colours. My heart sank more. Then, the last one she shook out was the floral two-piece in cobalt-blue and white, with two cute little tassels at the back.

'That's it!' I cried.

She checked the tag inside the back of the costume. 'It's the right size. Would you like to try it on?'

My heart was thumping as I went into the change room. I took off my T-shirt and shorts and put on the bikini. I looked in the mirror. It fit!

I pulled back the curtain and sashayed outside. Charlie, Meg and Cici were waiting with bated breath.

'It's adorable!' said Cici.

'Thank goodness,' said Meg.

'You look gorgeous,' said Charlie.

I spun around so the tassels twirled out.

'Anyone for a swim this afternoon?' I asked, my cheeks aching from smiling.

'Absolutely,' agreed the girls together.

It was the best feeling when I took that swimming costume up to the front counter. I peeled out the forty dollars from my wallet and my twenty-dollar gift voucher and piled them on top.

'I'll take this cossie, please,' I said.

The assistant behind the counter picked up my money and scanned the price tag.

'I recognise you,' she said, peering at me closely. 'You're Pippa, the girl who brought in the dog-walking poster a few days ago, aren't you?'

'Yes,' I said proudly.

'I've been meaning to ring you,' she said. 'I have two Jack Russells called Scruffy and Patch, and I wondered if you could walk them for me?'

I thought of the two naughty Jack Russells we'd seen digging at the park. I glanced at the other girls, then I beamed back at her.

'Sorry, I'm fully booked with dog-walking clients at the moment, but I'll let you know if I get a vacancy.'

'No problem,' she said, as she printed off

my receipt. 'Tell me if you know anyone else who walks dogs. It's hard to find responsible animal lovers to look after my cheeky Jack Russells.'

'Will do.' I grabbed the bag with my purchase and swung it high.

As we walked out of the shop, a man was strolling by pushing a double pram and leading a small black puppy. The puppy saw me and took off, racing towards us. The man was taken by surprise and dropped the lead. The puppy ran straight for me, then jumped up, licking my knees.

'Rufus,' I cried, catching hold of his red lead and giving him a good rub on the tummy. Rufus woofed with pleasure. 'Good boy.'

The man hurried over to us, looking embarrassed. 'I'm so sorry. Rufus is the worst escape artist.'

'I know,' I said. 'I'm Pippa, and I've been walking Rufus for the last few days.'

'Wufus berry naughty,' piped up a voice from the pram.

Then I realised who was in the pram. On one side, sitting up and waving his chubby fist at me, was Carlo. Lying next to him was a tiny baby, tucked up in a flannelette sheet.

'Anna had her baby,' I said, with delight. We all crowded around the pram to inspect the newborn. She was as bald as an egg with tiny starfish hands.

'This is Chiara Rose,' said the man, beaming with pride. 'And I'm Anna's husband – Matteo.'

'Welcome to the world, Chiara,' said Cici.

'Chiara Rose – that's such a pretty name,' said Charlie.

'How old is she?' asked Meg.

'She was born in the middle of the night on Thursday and we brought her back from hospital this morning,' explained Matteo. 'Anna's at home having a sleep.'

We all cooed and fussed over baby Chiara

until Carlo and Rufus became jealous and insisted on some attention of their own. Rufus barked loudly, pawing at my foot.

'Where's Mama?' wailed Carlo. 'I want Mama *now*.'

Chiara crumpled up her face and began to bellow.

'I'd better get home,' said Matteo, looking harried.

'Give our love to Anna,' I said. 'And tell her to call me if she ever needs Rufus to be walked.'

'Can you take him tomorrow?' asked Matteo.

'I'd love to,' I said.

CHAPTER 14

SLUMBER PARTY

Back at our new apartment, everything was finished. The girls and I walked through each room, admiring every detail. Our parents were sitting around the dining table drinking cups of tea and chatting. Mum's cheeks were pink with happiness as she sipped from a dainty china teacup. Summer was sniffing around under the table in case anyone dropped any crumbs.

We peered around the doorway into Bella's room. She was sprawled on her new rug with an entire army of dinosaurs, of all sizes and colours, covering most of the floor space.

'*Roaarrr*,' yelled Bella, as she made her tyrannosaurus devour her brachiosaur. The brachiosaur retaliated with a gnashing of teeth. Smudge dashed from where she was hiding under Bella's bed and ran for safety.

I rolled my eyes at the others, who giggled. I scooped up Smudge and stroked her to comfort her. She soon rumbled with contented purrs.

'Let's close the door,' I whispered. I shut Bella's door, and we could hardly hear the bellowing from inside. 'Aaah, blissful silence!'

Next, we checked out Harry's new bedroom. His stripy navy bed was neatly made and all his books were stacked on the shelves. His top hat and magician's cape were hung on a hook, while a large wooden chest held more of his magic paraphernalia. In the corner was the tall, black magic box, decorated with silver stars and moons, which he'd made with Papa for our school talent quest. I still don't know how he made Bella magically disappear, although it definitely didn't work with Smudge. I'd tried it.

'Have you seen this, Pippa?' asked Harry, his voice high-pitched with excitement.

Over near the window, on top of his chest of drawers, was a huge glass tank with red sand on the base, a large piece of twisted driftwood, a small rocky cave and something writhing around the foliage.

'Where did that come from?' I asked suspiciously. 'Is there something alive in there?'

'I've got a job too,' said Harry. 'I saw a notice in the window of the vet hospital, so I'm babysitting a pet python for a month, and I'm getting *paid* to do it. Papa and I have just picked him up.'

'A *snake*?' I asked, my heart racing. I peered into the tank. The python was black, patterned with creamy-yellow spots. Stretched out it looked about a metre and a half long. Its tongue flickered in and out as it slithered around the tank.

'Oh, great,' I moaned. 'Why didn't you just help me walk the dogs to earn some pocket money?'

'This is a much easier way to make money,' said Harry. 'I only have to feed him once a week and he exercises himself. He's a diamond python, and his name's –'

'Balthazar?' I interrupted him.

'Yes,' said Harry. 'How did you know?'

'I just guessed,' I said. 'Do we *have* to have a snake living with us in our new home?'

'Yep,' he replied. 'I was paid forty dollars for the month and I've already spent it all on crystals at the markets on the way home.'

Sure enough, Harry had his new collection of crystals, of all shapes and sizes, artfully arranged on his windowsill, where they could sparkle in the sunlight.

'I got white quartz, green quartz and rose quartz,' said Harry, picking up the coloured crystals and showing us one by one. 'This one's blue kyanite, that's citrine, that's selenite and this one's black tourmaline.'

Harry reverently picked up a rough round grey rock.

'But this one's *super* special,' he said. 'I could only afford a small one.'

'Really?' asked Cici, looking sceptical.

Harry snapped open the rock to reveal a wonderland of sparkling purple crystals clustered inside. 'It's an amethyst geode . . .'

'Oooh,' said Meg. 'That's amazing.'

'That's really cool, Harry,' I said. 'But do you think you could keep your bedroom door closed just in case Balthazar is an escape artist like Rufus? I don't want a diamond python exploring my room.'

'He's not venomous,' objected Harry.

'A bit slimy though,' said Cici, with a shudder of revulsion.

'No, he's not,' said Harry. 'Do you want me to get him out so you can hold him?'

'Maybe later,' I said firmly. 'We're going for a swim.'

Something Charlie had said made me think of a brilliant idea. I asked the girls to wait for me in my room while I went to ask Mum something special.

I pulled her aside into the kitchen.

'Mum, could I please have a sleepover tonight with the other girls?' I begged. 'In my new room? I've never been able to have them for a sleepover before.'

I had visions of the perfect Sassy Sister sleepover – staying up late, singing karaoke, dancing in our pyjamas, eating chocolate at midnight. What could be better?

For a moment I thought Mum was going to say no, but then she cuddled me close. 'I think you deserve a celebration with the girls, Pipkin. Luckily Eric brought us dinner, so we have heaps of food.'

I jumped for joy. 'Yay! Let me go and ask them right now.'

In the end, everyone's families stayed for dinner – Mimi and Papa, Nathalie and Eric, Mariana and Phillip, Jodie and Dave.

All the siblings came over as well – Will, Jack, Oscar, Seb, Sophia and Daisy. We played a big game of touch football on the beach before dinner. Then we washed the sand off, swimming in the cove as I rejoiced in my pretty new costume.

Papa cooked a big pot of his famous spaghetti bolognaise, Mimi made garlic bread and Mum tossed a green salad to go with Eric's spinach and ricotta cannelloni. For dessert we helped Cici bake some mini meringues, which we topped with whipped cream and raspberries.

The adults ate dinner upstairs in our living

room. They sat around the table Papa had built with the French doors wide open and candles flickering on the veranda.

The twelve kids sat on the jetty watching the sky and the sea change colours, from aqua to crimson and gold as the sun set behind the mountain. We snorted with laughter at Oscar's ridiculous jokes while we ate our Italian feast, followed by Cici's delicious raspberry mini pavlovas. Summer lay down next to me with her head in my lap, and I stroked her shaggy back. She whined with pleasure.

Down on the beach a group of four fire jugglers began practising. It was the same group I'd seen the other day in the park. The firesticks tumbled over and over in the air, creating fiery patterns against the twilight sky.

'A circus performance just for us,' I said. One juggler took a blazing sword and swallowed it, extinguishing the flame in his mouth. We all applauded.

'How does he do that?' asked Charlie.

'I'd like to try fire juggling,' said Harry.

'No way, Harry,' I said.

'And for our next performance,' said Cici, in her most theatrical voice, 'I give you dancing dolphins.' She pointed out towards the pink-streaked cove, where a pod of dolphins were swimming. One young dolphin jumped clear out of the water in a joyful gymnastic display.

'It's Jupiter showing off again,' said Meg proudly.

Charlie nudged me. 'A lucky sign for your new home, Pippa.'

I looked at my three beautiful best friends and thought about how hard they had worked to help us get here. I couldn't believe I'd been so jealous of them only a few days ago. I thought about what Zoe had said back then, and I realised she was right.

I *am* the luckiest girl on the planet.

CICI'S MINI RASPBERRY PAVLOVAS

Makes about 10

⅓ CUP OF CASTER SUGAR

2 EGG WHITES

300 ML OF THICKENED CREAM (OR CAN REPLACE WITH
THICK GREEK YOGHURT FOR A HEALTHIER SNACK)

HALF A PUNNET (125 GRAMS) OF RASPBERRIES

1. PRE-HEAT OVEN TO 150 DEGREES CELSIUS.
2. LINE TWO BAKING TRAYS WITH BAKING PAPER.
3. PLACE TWO EGG WHITES INTO A BOWL AND BEAT WITH
   ELECTRIC MIXER UNTIL SOFT PEAKS FORM.
4. GRADUALLY SPRINKLE IN CASTER SUGAR, ONE SPOONFUL
   AT A TIME, AND KEEP BEATING THE MIXTURE UNTIL SUGAR
   IS DISSOLVED AND THE PEAKS ARE THICK AND GLOSSY
   (THIS WILL TAKE AT LEAST FIVE MINUTES).

5. USE A HEAPED TABLESPOON TO PLACE DOLLOPS OF THE MIXTURE ONTO THE BAKING TRAYS. USE THE BACK OF THE SPOON TO FLATTEN EACH ONE INTO A ROUND MERINGUE.

6. BAKE FOR 20 MINUTES OR UNTIL CRISP.

7. OPEN THE OVEN DOOR AND ALLOW THE MERINGUES TO COOL COMPLETELY IN THE OVEN (ABOUT ONE HOUR).

8. IN A CLEAN BOWL, WHIP THICKENED CREAM.

9. WHEN READY TO SERVE, TOP EACH MERINGUE WITH A SPOONFUL OF WHIPPED CREAM OR YOGHURT AND DECORATE WITH RASPBERRIES. YOU CAN ALSO USE STRAWBERRIES, BLUEBERRIES, MANGO, KIWIFRUIT, PASSIONFRUIT OR A MIXTURE OF YOUR FAVOURITE FRUITS.

10. PERFECT FOR A SASSY SISTERS SLEEPOVER. ENJOY!

DON'T MISS OUT ON ANY OF
PIPPA'S ADVENTURES

COLLECT THEM ALL!

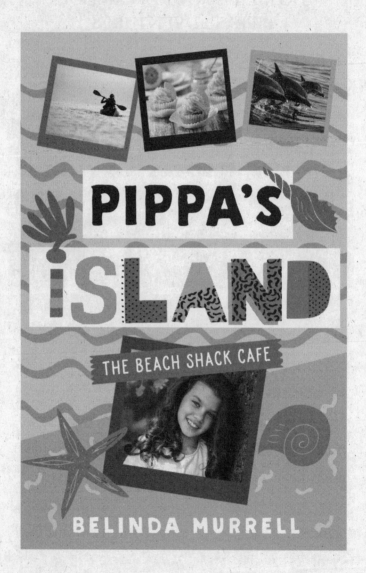

PIPPA'S iSLAND

THE BEACH SHACK CAFE

BELINDA MURRELL

THE BEACH SHACK CAFE

Pippa has just arrived at a new school, in a new town, and even living on a gorgeous island isn't cheering her up. Her arrival causes ripples at Kira Cove Primary School – but Pippa soon starts to make friends with eco-warrior Meg, boho-chick Charlie, and fashionista and cupcake baker Cici.

Pippa's mum plans to buy a rustic old boatshed and start a bookshop cafe, and Pippa worries they'll lose all their money in this madcap venture – until her new friends come to the rescue to help get the grand opening back on track.

Will Kira Island ever feel like home?

OUT NOW

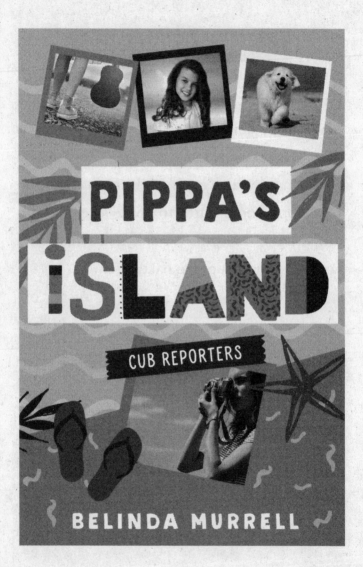

PIPPA'S iSLAND

CUB REPORTERS

BELINDA MURRELL

CUB REPORTERS

Pippa is settling in to her island home – she's even learning to surf. School is abuzz when Mrs Neill announces the launch of a new student newspaper. But how will Pippa, Meg, Charlie and Cici decide what to write about when the four friends have such different interests? A fashion photo shoot could be fun – if it weren't for bad weather, a naughty puppy and other disasters.

Just when things couldn't get any worse, the cub reporters get a news scoop that could bring the whole town together at the Beach Shack Cafe. Cupcakes for everyone!

Whose story will make the front page?

OUT NOW

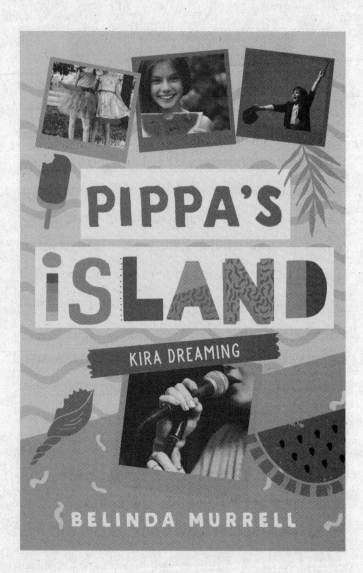

PIPPA'S iSLAND

KIRA DREAMING

BELINDA MURRELL

KIRA DREAMING

Kira Cove Public School is hosting a talent quest. Cici, Meg and Charlie couldn't be more excited to perform, but Pippa gets butterflies at the thought of singing on stage. After a disastrous audition the girls get a second chance, but can Pippa find a way to smash her stage fright before the VIP concert?

Meanwhile, at the Beach Shack Cafe a mysterious visitor is causing havoc when backs are turned. When Pippa finds a clue, she is determined to track down the mischievous cafe thief.

Will Pippa sing with the Sassy Sisters?

OUT NOW

PIPPA'S iSLAND

CAMP CASTAWAY

BELINDA MURRELL

CAMP CASTAWAY

The students in class 5M are heading off to school camp. Pippa has never been away on camp before, at least not to a deserted tropical island! The Sassy Sisters are looking forward to five blissful days together exploring Shipwreck Island's beaches and lagoon. But when the teams get regrouped, Pippa has to learn to cooperate with Olivia and the other girls.

Mrs Marshall promised challenges and adventure, but she forgot to mention the pranks. After one too many of the boys' tricks, the girls decide to take their revenge.

Will class 5M survive Camp Castaway?

OUT NOW

ABOUT THE AUTHOR

At about the age of eight, Belinda Murrell began writing stirring tales of adventure, mystery and magic in hand-illustrated exercise books. As an adult, she combined two of her great loves – writing and travelling the world – and worked as a travel journalist, technical writer and public relations consultant. Now, inspired by her own three children, Belinda is a bestselling, internationally published children's author. Her previous titles include four picture books, her fantasy adventure series, The Sun Sword

Trilogy, and her seven time-slip adventures, *The Locket of Dreams*, *The Ruby Talisman*, *The Ivory Rose*, *The Forgotten Pearl*, *The River Charm*, *The Sequin Star* and *The Lost Sapphire*.

For younger readers (aged 6 to 9), Belinda has the Lulu Bell series about friends, family, animals and adventures growing up in a vet hospital.

Belinda lives in Manly in a gorgeous old house overlooking the sea with her husband, Rob, her three beautiful children, Sammy the Stimson's python and her dog, Rosie. She is an Author Ambassador for Room to Read and Books in Homes.

Find out more about Belinda at her website: **www.belindamurrell.com.au**

Adventures are more fun with friends!
There are thirteen gorgeous Lulu Bell
stories for you to discover.

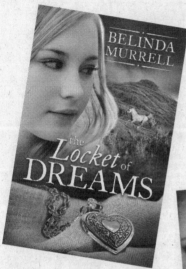

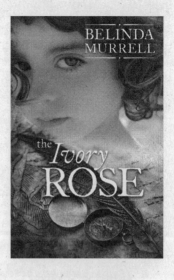

Love history? Escape to another time
with Belinda's seven beautiful
time-slip adventures.

If you love fantasy stories, you'll love
Belinda's Sun Sword trilogy.